BOOK THREE

# Rage

## A DARK MAFIA ROMANCE

# CHELLE ROSE

# NOTE TO THE READER

Your mental health is important. Please don't read blind if you have any triggers!

# DEDICATION:

To all the people who ever called a victim a liar.
FUCK YOU!
May you rot in hell with Leo.

# Prologue
## RAINA

The rules for women in our world are simple, but strict.

Rule #1 Your virginity is everything. Without it, you have no value.

Rule #2 Do as you're told.

Rule #3 Women are to be seen and not heard. If your input is desired, it will be demanded of you.

I was only eight years old when I learned I had only one role, as a girl born into our organization. Once I reached legal age, I'd be married, granting my father money and power. Sold like livestock. One day, I'd be forced to hand over my virginity to a man I would have no choice in marrying, so that I could give him an heir. A man that would be like my Uncle Leo, and take what he wanted, without ever considering what it would do to me.

Leo would never take my virginity, I knew that, but he took everything else.

*My innocence.*

*My heart.*

*My soul.*

Leo is where all good things go to die. And every time he touched me, I wanted to die. I tried more than once, and that's how I learned how to survive. The pain from the cut silences his voice. His touch. The harsh sting makes the demons lie dormant for a little while.

We are all born, and we all die. It's the one guarantee in life. I'm not afraid of what waits for me after this life, because I was born into hell. It can't be worse than this.

After building up the courage, I told my father what Leo had done to me. I was met with disbelief. Not his brother. I was branded as a liar in my own family. There's something about not being believed that's almost worse than the abuse. Worse than the feeling of his fingers on my skin. I had to prove it, and that's what I was going to do.

I clutch the results of the lie detector test in my hands as my driver approaches my driveway. Now my father will believe me, and make him stop. A smile graces my lips as I walk inside my house, straight to my father's office, joy filling me, knowing he'll never touch me again.

I knock lightly on his closed door, waiting to open it until he yells for me to enter.

I swallow hard as Leo turns to leave, and stares at me with a smirk.

"Be a good girl, Principessa."

I stand frozen as he walks around me, and I dig my nails into my wrist as hard as I can.

*Relief.*

It's not until he closes the door that I'm able to breathe again. I blink fast, trying to stop the tears threatening to fall, as I step forward and place the, now wrinkled, paper on my father's desk.

"What is this, Raina?" He asks, without looking away from his computer screen.

"Lie detector results."

With an arched brow, his gaze snaps to mine.

"What?"

"This is proof that what I said about Uncle Leo is true."

He sighs audibly, like I'm nothing more than an inconvenience, and nods to the chair in front of his desk.

8

"Sit."

I do as I'm told, because I always do as he says. That is my role, after all, as a girl.

He doesn't bother looking at the paper, instead he stares at me with disgust.

"Did he take your virginity?"

I shake my head no, because that's the only thing he hasn't taken from me.

"Good. Then we don't have a problem. You're a beautiful girl, Raina. Men will want you. I can't blame him, really. As long as your virginity is intact for your future husband, there's no issue."

I lose the fight then, and the tears fall, but he doesn't care. His words have proven the one thing I tried hard to forget. He doesn't care about me. Like a cow bought to be sold for its meat, that's my only worth. My vagina is the only part of me with any value. Of course, as long as it's saved for my future husband that I don't want.

"If I weren't a virgin, I wouldn't be forced to marry?"

My father narrows his gaze at me, clearly understanding my thought process.

"No, because dead girls don't marry."

The silence stretches between us, and he turns back to his computer.

"If there's nothing else, I have work to do."

# Chapter One
## KAGE

I sit in my club, watching the girls dance in their cages, as Psycho sits across from me, opening and closing his knife, and getting on my last fucking nerve.

"She hasn't come to talk to you?"

My attention snaps to him.

"Who?"

"Stop looking at your fucking whores and listen to me. The new Assistant District Attorney."

I shake my head no before saying, "Not yet. Bones said there was a new one, but he didn't say anything else."

Touching the tip of his knife, he growls with obvious anger.

"She is trying to make a name for herself, and apparently her way of doing that is going after our family."

We have most of law enforcement, including the prosecutor's office, in our pocket. A do-gooder is dangerous for us, because they can't be bought. As a mafia family, the only legitimate businesses we are involved in are fronts. This club, for example. I use it to launder money, although I do rather enjoy the cage dancers. There's something about a half naked woman trapped within the bars that does it for me. Who am I kidding? Anyone trapped in a cage fills me with a joy it shouldn't.

Keeping a person caged like an animal is intoxicating. The wide eyes, the rapid heart rate, the way they glance around, hoping for a way to escape, before they accept there is none. The begging, screaming, crying. It's a high I've never gotten from a drug.

"Kill her."

The solution is obvious to me, and I have no idea why Psycho hasn't already done it.

He glares at me as he licks the small amount of blood from his blade.

"Why haven't I thought of that?" He rolls his eyes like I'm an idiot.

"Bones told me not to, and I quote, 'touch a hair on her head'."

Leaning forward, I pour us both another couple of shots of whiskey.

I pick mine up and take a gulp, as Psycho downs his drink in an instant.

"This is why I should've been the head of the family. Bones thinks too much."

Focusing on my drink, I don't respond, because anything I say will make him see red, more than he already is.

My father made many mistakes, most of them involving our youngest sibling, Reaper. Putting Bones at the head of our organization, instead of Psycho, was not a mistake. If he said not to kill the new ADA, there's a reason. Bones does very little without having solid thought behind it.

He rises from his chair, clearly done with our conversation.

"Where are you going?"

With a vicious grin, he says, "I've got a guy I've been torturing for a week. I think he's probably ready for round three. Besides, you're probably ready to get your dick sucked, and I don't want to be around to watch that."

I chuckle at everything he said. Fucking Psycho. I've seen his method of torture enough times to know it by heart.

*Cut. Watch them bleed. Stitch them up. Rinse and repeat.*

My oldest brother is a fan of blood. The rest of us can live with or without it. For Psycho, though, it's not a want, it's a need. He craves it, like a thirsty man wandering the desert craves water. He was right though, I'm ready for a blow job.

It's not about the girl, it's about the release, so it doesn't matter who she is. Katrina has been eyeing me all night, with her pleading brown eyes. She'll do. I motion her over and she knows the drill, immediately dropping to her knees. I groan in frustration as my phone rings, vibrating on the table. Of course, the name Bones flashes across the screen. Every fucking time. I swear my brother is the biggest cock blocker on the planet.

"What?" I growl as I answer, my cock in Katrina's throat while she stares at me, wondering if she should continue.

"Get over to the house. We have a problem."

I roll my eyes and, as if he can see me, he says, "Now, Kage. This is not a fucking request." Before I have a chance to respond, he disconnects the call.

"Sorry, sweetheart. Next time."

Getting up off her knees, she looks at me with those big *Bambi* eyes.

"Call me."

I chuckle as I zip my pants up and head out of my club. We both know she'd love it if I called her, and we both know I won't. Women in our world are disposable. I will die a bachelor, getting my dick sucked by random women. I don't hide the man I am. They know. I'm a pig and I'm okay with it. I'll never be the man that my brothers Bones and Reaper have turned into. Monogamy is for pussies. It's something I'll never understand, and I have no intention of trying to.

I roll up to Bones' house and quickly park before heading to the door. Kissing my sister-in-law Athena on the cheek, I go to his office, where I know he's waiting.

Opening the door, I see that my other brothers are already here, and Bones scowls at me.

"It's about fucking time you grace us with your presence."

13

I take a seat on the black leather couch beside Psycho, and roll my eyes.

"Sorry for the delay, Master."

Psycho snorts and chuckles beside me, while Bones flashes me a death glare.

"Don't fucking start, Kage. I'm pissed off enough as it is."

We all sit quietly, waiting for him to tell us what the problem is. Judging by the tic in his jaw, there is one, beyond my asshole behavior. Reaper sits on the other side of Psycho, and asks, "What happened?"

"One of our shipments was intercepted."

I ask, "What was taken?"

He rubs his temples as he answers me, "AR-15s."

"Fuck," we all respond in unison.

Psycho asks, "Do we have any leads?"

He nods slowly, with a glint in his eye, and I know someone is dying today, but not before my brother breaks some bones.

"We need to go to Warehouse seven, and have a little chat with Gino and his crew."

# Chapter Two
## KAGE

We pull up to the front of the warehouse, and I smile to myself, because we aren't trying to hide our presence. By the time we reach our guys working here, they'll be shaking in their boots. Most of the time, only one of us shows up to check on things. If we're all here, they know they're in serious trouble.

As we walk in, panic crosses Gino's face, but he quickly schools it. He has learned the hard way to not show fear. Fear means guilt in his case. Bones walks over to him, with slow measured steps, and a gleam in his eyes.

"Gino. Would you care to explain the missing containers?"

His eyes dart to his men, who are showing far more fear than Gino is, before returning his gaze to my brother.

"Boss, I don't know anything about stolen shipments."

Bones lowers his head, his face an inch from Gino's, and bares his teeth with a growl.

"You're not only a thief, but a liar. I've seen the video. Now, where the fuck are my weapons?"

Psycho and Reaper approach on either side of him, their expressions no less menacing than the man in front of him.

He trembles, as I enjoy the show.

We frequently have traitors among us, but this is how the ones that haven't gotten their hands dirty learn to keep them clean. I barely hide my chuckle as Psycho takes his hand, and points to each of his fingers.

"Eeny, meeny, miny," he sing-songs in an evil tone.

Bones repeats himself, "Where the fuck are my weapons?"

Gino shakes his head emphatically.

"I don't know, Boss. It wasn't me."

Psycho growls, "Moe," and slices off Gino's middle finger.

The frantic scream that comes from Gino is almost funny, because it's going to get a lot worse for him.

Bones calls for me.

"Kage, talk to the others."

By 'talk', he means to get answers at any cost. I smile as I walk over to the first group of men, and crack my knuckles while I whistle. It's a trait we share. We all have similarities, although our youngest brother is the only actual serial killer. Bones, Psycho, and I may not go out searching for people to kill, but we won't shy away from it either. And we don't hate it.

As an organization, we never tolerate theft, but when it's a trusted employee, it burns differently. And that means the punishment is far more harsh. Death comes regardless, but it's more prolonged when it's a traitor.

I stare at the three men in front of me, as they tremble with terror.

"Would you like to go home unharmed to your families?"

They all nod in unison.

"Tell me what you know."

The men on the left and right both shake their heads, swearing they don't know anything, but the one in the middle... he knows something. Fear has a stench that most people don't realize. It reeks of sweat and soiled clothing.

"Gustavo."

Reluctantly, he lifts his head and meets my gaze.

"Do you want to go home to that beautiful wife of yours? Or do you wish to die alongside Gino?"

"I wan-t-t to go home," he stammers as he attempts to look calm, but is anything but.

Out of the corner of my eye, I spot Psycho slicing off another one of Gino's fingers, with his custom blade. This one is a honesuki, some sort of Japanese steel that he went on and on about when he got it. I didn't really care but I remember something about it cutting through bone and now I see he wasn't stretching the truth.

"Unless you wish to join Gino, I suggest you tell me what you know."

A tear rolls down his cheek as he rats out his best friend.

"I didn't do it. I told him not to. He needed the money, so he organized it."

I nod my understanding.

"Who has our weapons, Gustavo? You won't get another chance to answer me."

Bones is listening closely, as Psycho tortures Gino, one digit at a time. Bones is always aware of what's happening around him. It's one of his gifts, paying attention when it appears he isn't.

"The Abruzzos. They helped him steal them, and gave him money. I don't know how much, but it was a lot."

I smirk at him.

"Good job. Let today serve as a reminder of what happens to our men that betray us. Sorry for your loss."

This will not be the last time we deal with a situation like this. I can almost guarantee the men in this warehouse that live, will never make the grave mistake Gino has. For them, this will be a hard lesson learned. Don't fuck with the Bonettis. I'm not delusional though. There will be some pathetic sack not here today that will be offered millions of dollars to betray us. It's the same reason people rob banks, knowing the chances of getting away with it are slim. The thought will always be in the back of their heads.

*What if I can get away with it?*

That simple thought is what gets them killed, because they never do. We will always find out. It's not if, it's when.

I walk back over to Bones, and we watch Psycho make Gino scream like it's a horror movie we've seen a thousand times, with boredom.

"I assume you heard."

17

He nods slowly and barks at Psycho.

"I'm going home to my butterfly. If you want to play with him, then take him to your basement."

Not a word is said about the Abruzzos, but I know it's coming. We will get our weapons back, with the added bonus of their lives.

# Chapter Three

## RAINA

It seems lately that every week means another funeral. Three of my six brothers are dead, all due to the Bonettis, a rival family with no moral compass. Most people would say any mafia family is lacking in integrity, and mostly they aren't wrong, but some of them are worse than others. The fact that this all started over a parking spot is unbelievable. My brother Vincenzo is dead because he dared to park in Nico Bonetti's parking spot. And that asshole decided that one spot was important enough to start a mob war. *Fucking idiot.*

Now Tony is also dead, and my father is losing his grip. He isn't responding like a mafia Don should, or normally would. He's breaking as his sons get picked off one by one. The tension in our home is palpable, as my mother cries endlessly, and my father comes unglued.

Two of my three dead brothers were at the Bonetti club when they were killed. It's something I've never understood. Why would you go to your enemy's place and expect this to not happen? They allow rival families in, without weapons, and they aren't allowed in the VIP area. Knowing the Bonettis are armed, but you are not, seems awfully risky to me. I've always thought that was asking for trouble, however, as a woman, my opinion is not valued or listened to at all.

*"Raina, a good mob wife knows her place."*

I've heard it more times than I can count, and every time my mother says it, I want to stab myself in the fucking eardrums. Maybe she's fine with a life like that, but I'm not. I'll never be the good wife that does whatever my husband says, which is why I am not marrying Gabriel Ferrari, as my parents have mentioned several times. I will run, and they'll never see me again, before that happens.

Normally, dinner time is filled with chatter, but tonight it's the complete opposite. The three empty chairs are blatantly obvious, more so than an empty seat would usually be. My mother's gaze bounces between them, while my father grips his fork so hard, I wonder if he's going to injure himself. My three brothers eat silently, and I know all of us are wondering the same thing. Which of us is next on the Bonettis' hit list. Reaper Bonetti specifically. We don't know if they were targeted because of who they are, because this asshole is a serial killer, and will kill anybody for no reason, but three from the same family cannot be a coincidence.

My father addresses my remaining brothers; Edoardo, Aldo, and Rocco.

"If I find out any of you is at that fucking club, there will be hell to pay. Why my sons are handing money over to Bonetti scum is beyond me. There are other places to drink and find pussy."

My mother makes a face, like she just bit into a sour lemon, because what my father said bothered her, yet she's a good mafia wife, so she wouldn't dare say a word to him.

I roll my eyes as I stab at a piece of chicken on my plate, and my father notices.

"Something to say, Raina?"

Shaking my head, I say, "No, father."

While I have a lot to say, I know better, especially when he's on edge.

He turns to Rocco. "Everything set with the girl?"

My mother and I exchange worried glances, but stay silent while listening to their conversation.

Rocco chuckles obnoxiously.

"Bella, almost Bonetti, is pregnant with Reaper's baby. I will bring her to you tomorrow."

My mother gasps loudly.

"Gio. Not the baby."

He arches an eyebrow at her and growls.

"Silence. They killed three of your babies. Why should any of them survive? Next will be the head Bonetti's child, Atlas. We will kill every fucking one of them, and the wives too."

My mother hangs her head down, but doesn't say anything further. Her saying anything at all was surprising, because she never speaks unless spoken to. My father doesn't hit her, but he definitely controls her, and I don't blame him entirely, because she allows it. By doing everything he says, and never questioning him, she consents to it. It's not entirely her fault though, because it's how our family has always been. It seems I'm the only one that has a problem with it. I knew, the second the words came out of Rocco's mouth though, that it would be upsetting to my mother. I had seven brothers, but the firstborn was killed by a rival family, and my mother has never recovered. She has always thought children should be left out of adult fights.

*We don't send babies into wars. Why should they be casualties?*

I don't disagree with her, but again, it doesn't matter what we think. If my father has decided Reaper's baby is to die, it will. We can't save anyone other than ourselves.

My father glances at Edoardo.

"Everything set up?"

He nods.

"Yes, the basement is ready with the tools you requested."

His face shows the first grin I've seen since this started, but it's pure evil.

"Perfect. I'll cut that fucking demon out of her, and send a picture to the Bonettis as a warning."

Is my father an idiot? He might be, because that's not going to make them back down. If anything, it's going to cause more carnage, not less. They are not going to lose two family members and do nothing. I am sure my father doesn't intend for this Bella woman to survive. I have tried to keep my mouth shut, but he's playing with all our lives, so I can't keep quiet.

21

"You do know they will retaliate? They aren't going to back down after your warning. You are going to kill one of their women, and an innocent child. If anything, you are escalating this war. Cutting a child from its mother's stomach?"

I shake my head with disgust before continuing.

"That's not retaliation, it's heinous, worse than anything a Bonetti has ever been accused of."

He glares at me, and I rise from my seat before he speaks, because I know his words before he even opens his mouth.

"Go to your room, Raina. Now!"

"She's right, Gio," my mother says as I exit the dining room. For a moment, my chest swells with pride that my mother spoke up, however briefly. Maybe she'll be sent to her room for being disobedient as well.

# Chapter Four

## KAGE

My little brother Reaper's wedding is in three days, so when he calls me at five in the morning, I'm sure it's about that, which pisses me off. He continually asks me for advice about women, even though I don't know jack shit about them. I like to fuck them, but beyond that, I know squat. I answer the call, intending for him to hear my annoyance.

"What the fuck do you want, Reaper?"

His voice comes out shaky, and instantly alerts me that something is very wrong.

"Kage. They-"

Is he fucking hyperventilating?

"Reaper, breathe. What's going on, brother?"

I can hear through the phone as he attempts to take a deep breath.

"They took her. Kage, they have Bella."

Once again, he's calling me, when he should be calling my older brother, and head of our family, Bones, but I won't turn him away.

"Who?"

"The Abruzzos," he growls, his voice reverberating with so much pain.

"Get to Bones. I'll meet you there. Have your driver take you."

We hang up, and I put my coffee cup away and go upstairs to get dressed. I call my brother Psycho on my way.

"What?" He growls, sounding as annoyed as I was, when my phone rang early this morning.

"Meet me at Bones' house. The Abruzzos have Bella and, as you can imagine, Reaper is losing his fucking mind."

"Fuck," he says, but I also know he's smiling, or at least will be. Not because our little brother's girl has been taken, but because he knows he gets to see some action today. The only one in our family that enjoys killing more than our serial killer little brother is Psycho. The way he kills isn't bloodless like our youngest brother. It's prolonged and brutal. If the Abruzzos have Bella, it will not end quickly or painlessly. One thing is guaranteed. The suffering will be great. Women will not be spared. If they are in that house when we get there, they will die.

The Bonetti men are not what you'd call good, by any stretch of the imagination. If you're going to be bad, you better be good at it. And we are. There's nothing we do better than protecting our own, and the moment Reaper decided Bella was his, she became ours. That baby she is carrying has part Bonetti blood running through its tiny veins. If anything happens to his child before we get there, my little brother is going to kill everything that moves, Abruzzo or not. Reaper isn't what most people would label as mentally stable to begin with. Bones has managed to keep him somewhat in line. However, losing Bella, and his baby, will push him over the edge.

I finish getting dressed, and head to my brother's house as quickly as I can, which means speeding. Luckily for me, I don't have to worry about the police attempting to pull me over. Being a Bonetti has its perks, and owning the higher ups in the police department is only one of many.

Swerving in and out traffic, I ignore the blaring horns as I chuckle to myself. If they knew who I was, there wouldn't be a single one, but I'll let it go, because I have bigger fish to fry.

*The fucking Abruzzos.*

I know they're pissed about my brother killing three of their sons, and I don't blame them at all. Going after the women of the family is fucking weak. Real men go after the true target, not what they perceive as incapable of defending themselves. I can't help but chuckle to myself, as I pull into my brother's driveway, because Bella isn't like Athena, or any other mafia woman I've ever met. If she isn't restrained one hundred percent of the time, we may show up to find a lot of dead bodies.

As I park my Escalade, I spot Reaper's Range Rover, as well as Psycho's Outlander, and decide I better get my ass inside, before my youngest brother loses his goddamn mind. I don't particularly understand his obsession with Bella, any more than I can comprehend Bones with Athena. Both of my brothers are fucking psychotic over their women, whereas I have never met a woman I could stomach to keep around for longer than two days. Once I fuck them, it's over. The best part is the anticipation, but once that's done, so are we. Wanting to be inside the same woman for the rest of your life? I don't fucking think so. I'm not sure what the hell happened to those two, but it'll never happen to me. Reaper, I kind of understand, because he was a virgin when he met Bella. Bones, though? I don't know what the hell happened to him.

I walk into my brother's home and make my way through the entryway, while Athena tries to comfort Reaper. They sit on the sofa, talking between themselves, while Bones stands next to Psycho, not taking his eyes off his wife. He trusts Reaper; he knows our little brother loves her like a sister, but this is his way. Bones only looks away from her when he doesn't have a choice. It's fucking weird if you ask me, but whatever.

"What's the plan?" I ask, as I stand beside Bones.

He doesn't acknowledge me, but his wife.

"Butterfly."

She immediately gets up and goes over to him, and he kisses her on the forehead, speaking low, but I can still hear him.

"Go upstairs with Atlas."

"Luca," she complains.

He shakes his head and narrows his gaze at her.

"We have a child now. I need you to stay away from danger for him, if not for yourself."

She nods with a long drawn-out sigh.

"Please be careful, Luca. We need you."

"I promise," he says before he kisses her softly.

"I love you, Butterfly. I'll be back as soon as possible."

She turns to walk away but throws over her shoulder.

"I love you too, Luca."

Psycho grimaces as he shakes his head, making me bite my lip to not laugh.

"Fuck. That was disgusting. Can we go kill these assholes now?" Psycho asks.

Bones glares at him.

"Take a fucking seat, Psycho. We aren't storming in there, without everybody knowing what the hell we are doing."

He rolls his eyes, but takes a seat beside Reaper, and I walk over and sit on the other side of my youngest brother.

Bones pulls a remote out of his pocket, and a screen comes down from the ceiling, with a picture of a large house on it.

"This is the Abruzzo compound. It's much larger than Frank's mansion, where we found Bella last time. This isn't confirmed, but I'm told this crazy asshole has explosives along the perimeter of his home, and if he thinks he can't win, he'll blow it up. So we're going to be extra careful, because I'm not prepared to make my wife a widow. Understood?"

Psycho and I both nod, but Reaper sits on the couch, bouncing his knee while running his hand through his hair. He was fucked up last time she was taken, but this is worse. Maybe because of the baby. He looks like he might break into a thousand fucking pieces at any moment.

"Reaper. You with us?" Bones asks, as gently as he's probably capable of right now.

"Yeah, I get it. Alright? While you drone on about your safety shit, my girl and our baby are having god knows what done to them. I knew I should've gone by myself. You're going to cost me everything."

Bones sighs audibly.

"Let's get through this, and we can go get Bella."

He points to the picture on the screen.

"The front door leads to an entryway, that goes to a kitchen and living room. There's another of each on the second floor. The third floor is all offices. But through this garden," he points to the side of the property before continuing, "This leads to an outside basement. Inaccessible from inside the house. If I were a betting man, I'd put money on it that Bella is here."

Reaper groans loudly. "Fuck."

All four of us know the kind of shit that happens in basements. Nothing good. We come by that knowledge, because the terrible things that take place down there are things we have all probably done. None of us are saints, by any stretch of the imagination. At the end of the day, it doesn't really matter where they keep her. We know she isn't being treated well, if she's even alive. If they really want to make Reaper pay for what he's done, she probably isn't. In our world, you don't kill three men in one family and live to tell about it. My brother is a lethal man that few want to go up against. So it's not really surprising they didn't come after him, because the fact is, the Abruzzos are weak. Their only chance is to hurt women, and get my brother where he's vulnerable. This is the most powerless he'll be. Bella makes him weak and everybody knows it. The same goes with Bones having a wife.

"The De Lucas will not be joining us because they have other commitments, but if we need help, an acquaintance, Max, and his team of assassins are on standby. I am confident we can handle this on our own. We're going to start here and try to get her out. These men are no match for us, but given enough time, they are brutal with women. So priority number one is to get Bella out. Then we will teach them a lesson about fucking with what's ours."

We rise and follow him to the door. All of us are dressed in black pants, and black button-down shirts, including Reaper, which is a change.

Once we get to the vehicle we are taking, Bones' brand new Range Rover, he opens the back and hands us all bullet-proof vests, and weapons. He turns to Psycho with a narrowed gaze.

"I know you prefer knives. Just fucking humor me, okay? I want everybody armed with more than they need."

I don't think we've ever worn a vest, so that tells me he's concerned about this more than normal. None of us question it, because Bones is the boss. Even Psycho keeps his mouth shut. He should've been the head of the family after our father died, but it was handed to Bones because Psycho is an uncontrolled asshole, much like Reaper. Psycho still gives Bones a hard time occasionally, but this isn't the time for that, and even he knows that. We pile into the vehicle and Bones drives off, clearly knowing where he's going. I know the Abruzzos unfortunately, but I've never been to their home. Even before Reaper started killing the sons, we weren't exactly friends. Yet it was my brother's carelessness that put us in this situation. Bones is the only one complaining though, because while we might not be serial killers like Reaper, we do enjoy it.

# Chapter Five
## RAINA

I stand in my garden admiring the hard work I've put into it over the last three years. The pink roses are my favorite, and they're coming along so nicely. I also planted lavender, alliums, geraniums, and marigolds. I have vegetables on the other side, but the flowers are my favorite. This is my peaceful place. Nobody comes out here other than me, so I'm surprised when I see my brothers, father, and a few of their men, traipsing through the pavement that separates my two gardens. They aren't alone. There's a young blonde woman with them, and as they come closer, I notice her hands are zip tied behind her back. The panic is visible in her wide eyes, trembling bottom lip, and tears streaking her cheeks. The way she looks at me, it's like she thinks I can save her, and I can't. I know that, but her only words to me make my chest squeeze painfully.

"Please save my baby."

She isn't begging for her life. Her unborn child is her only concern, but they are currently one. Even if the baby had been born, I can't help her. Nobody will listen to me.

Rocco lifts his gun and hits her on the head with the butt of it.

"Shut up, cunt."

They yank her to the basement, and I know I'll probably never see this woman again. My only hope is that they kill her quickly, even though I know that's not their style. All three of my remaining brothers are into torture. They don't just like it; it gets them off. This Bella woman will pay for Reaper Bonetti's wrongs, and then they will come for us, and we'll all pay for my brothers', as well as my father's, actions. It's the mafia way. It's not *if* they come for us, it's when.

I want to save her, as I listen to her screams before the door closes. Yet, I know I can't. All three of my brothers will have no problem beating me black and blue, but Rocco is the worst of them. He will kill me without thinking twice. He is the sole reason I know what she'll be subjected to. The brutality. If Reaper and his brothers get here before she's dead, she won't be the woman she used to be. My brother changes women.

I stand staring at the door, willing it to open so the poor woman can escape. Of course, I don't have any superpowers, so I'm surprised when it opens, and Edoardo walks out and closes it behind him. He walks over to me, and glances at my flowers before looking back at me.

All of my brothers look alike; tall, with dark hair, and dark eyes. None of them are kind, but Eddie is probably the closest to it.

He narrows his gaze at me.

"Don't do anything stupid, alright? You know what Rocco is capable of, and I don't think Mama could handle losing you right now."

I blink back the unshed tears in my eyes.

"They're raping her, aren't they?"

He nods.

"Yeah, all three of them. As you know, that's not my game, so I left. You should go inside the house. You don't need to be here for this."

I shake my head in disgust at my brothers, and my father. It's my father that disappoints me the most. One might think a husband would be faithful to his wife, but dear old dad never has been. The basement is his playground. He fucks and kills whatever he wants with zero cares. There's no humanity to him, and it's that very reason, when the Bonettis come to kill us, that I hope he goes first, and I get to watch. I know what Edoardo said is true, he does not rape women, but he will torture them. My brother can pretend to be

30

better than the other men in my family, but I know he'll go back in there and hurt her.

Turning away from my brother, I do as he suggested and walk back to the house. I find my mother sipping tea in the dining room, and I sit across from her.

"They are raping her, Mama. All three of them."

She doesn't look at me, her gaze stays on her tea as if she's waiting for it to do something enthralling, or maybe it already is.

"Of course they are. Did you expect anything different, Raina?"

I slam my hands down on the table as I yell at her.

"Does this not fucking bother you?"

She lifts her gaze to mine and shakes her head.

"Do not curse at me. I may not get respect from anyone else in this house, but from you, I will. We are women, Raina. They do not care what we think or say. It is best to let it go, unless you'd like to take her place. Your blood will not save you. It'll be over in a few days."

My father has controlled her for their entire marriage, so I try to understand why she is the way she is, but it infuriates me. I can't do anything, and neither can she, I know that, but she could at least show some emotion, instead of being so detached.

I scoot my chair back and glare at my mother.

"And you wonder why I don't want children? Do you think I'd want to bring anything innocent into this family? Risk having a girl, so she could go through the same thing I have? Maybe worse? You keep asking why. *This* is fucking why!"

I storm off to my bedroom, before she has the chance to scold me for being so brazen as to say the 'F' word. My brothers are in the basement, raping, and brutally torturing, a woman because she has a connection to the Bonettis, and she is worried about my language? This family is fucked up beyond reason, and I only wish I could get out of it.

I could. There's nothing stopping me from running far away, and starting a new life, except her. My mother is my world, and while she pisses me off, I'd never leave her. Not willingly.

For tonight, I need to get the hell out of this house. I cannot stay here knowing what's happening in the basement. I wish I could disconnect myself from everything, the way my mother does, but I can't. So it's best for me to not be here. If I stay, and keep thinking about what they are doing to that woman, I'll do something stupid, and get myself killed.

I send a text to my best friend, Casey.

**Me:** *Meet me at the club. I have to get out of here.*

**Casey:** *Everything alright?*

**Me:** *I'll explain when I see you. Family is being family.*

There won't be any further questions, so I set my phone down so I can get ready. Casey knows when I say, 'family is being family', that there's some nasty mafia shit going down. We met when we were in high school, and have been inseparable since that day. For years, people expected us to date, but we've always only been friends. I never had an interest in more than that, and if he did, he never expressed it. Although his distaste for my family's business might have had more than a little to do with it.

After getting dressed, in black leather pants and a matching sleeveless shirt, I apply my eye makeup for the evening, when the sound of heavy footfalls echoes through the hallway outside my bedroom door. As calmly as possible, I set my brush on my dressing table and move underneath it, and adjust the sheer curtain so it's covering me. It's a black material, so it'll conceal me a bit if no one looks too closely. My heart pounds in my chest as I squeeze my eyes closed tight. *Mama.* I don't care if they kill everyone in this hellhole, as long as she survives.

The footsteps stop, and my bedroom door clicks loudly, as muffled voices penetrate the quiet space. I stop breathing and wait.

# Chapter Six
## KAGE

We have men searching the house, but we know where Bella is, from her screams alone. I glance at Bones and Reaper, who are talking quietly. I know our youngest brother is getting instructions on remaining calm, before we charge into this basement. Once we get the nod from Bones, we move through the door, down the dingy steps, moving the cobwebs away that touch our hair, and follow the sound of Bella's cries. I glance at Reaper, and the pain in his expression is hard to look at. This is the reason I'll never get hung up on a woman. It's fucking dangerous. In our line of work, deadly. The strongest woman is still a weakness. Even a badass one like my future sister-in-law.

Turning the corner, we find her with two men fucking her over a table, and another holds her down while his brother holds a knife, cutting into her stomach as she sobs. The sound that comes from my brother is one I've never heard from him. Pure anguish.

Bones quickly takes control.

"Let go of my sister. Now."

Reaper clenches his fists, clearly having trouble letting Bones take the lead. There's no doubt my brother wants to be the one to choke the life out of them, but he has bigger issues right now.

*Bella, and their child.*

The three men step away from her. The head of the family, Giovanni Abruzzo, and his son, Rocco, stand there with their dicks exposed pathetically. Aldo glances at the man in charge, like he is going to save the day, when there's no chance of that happening.

"Reaper, get Bella to the hospital. Psycho, get six men to pick up Athena, and take her to the hospital with him."

Glancing at the Abruzzos, he says, "Do up your fucking pants before I cut your tiny dicks off."

They are quick to do as they're told. It's interesting how they want to brutalize a woman, but now they stand like cowards.

Reaper lifts a bleeding Bella into his arms and races off with her, while speaking in a low voice meant only for her. I think her need for medical attention is the only thing holding him together at the moment.

Psycho moves to leave, but Bones stops him.

"Make sure they know if anything happens to my wife, they'll pay with their lives. Not a fucking hair on her head better be harmed."

My oldest brother rolls his eyes and grumbles, "Got it," as he heads off to do what Bones instructed him to.

Neither Psycho nor myself understand this fixation our brothers have on their women. I enjoy pussy as much as any other man, but I've never had one that I say, 'gee, I'd like to fuck only this one for the rest of my life'. It's insane the way both Bones and Reaper are with their women. Not long after Reaper became obsessed with Bella, Psycho and I made a pact to never lose our fucking minds over a woman. No matter how much we like fucking them. Psycho, being the asshole he is, promised to stab me if I ever go back on my word. I won't.

Bones points to the floor and addresses the Abruzzos.

"On your knees."

Papa Abruzzo chuckles obnoxiously.

"I don't think so."

I'm thoroughly entertained as I watch my brother glare at him.

"I know so. Get on your fucking knees."

His sons are the first to follow the command, and drop to their knees on the hard uneven basement floor.

The old man is more resistant, but eventually caves, like we knew he would, with a little help, of course. I swing my leg up and give

36

him one hard kick to the kneecaps, causing him to fall with a loud thud, and an even more audible scream.

Bones chuckles to himself.

"I guess you should've listened the first time."

Stepping closer to them, I narrow my gaze at the father.

"Why did you cut into her stomach?"

My question is met with silence, which only annoys me further.

I glance at one of his sons, Edoardo, and raise an eyebrow. He shakes his head, like this wasn't his plan and he's disgusted, but that doesn't matter. He will die, the same as the others, even though he was merely watching.

"He wanted to cut her baby out."

She isn't far along, so I don't understand.

"The baby isn't old enough to survive outside its mother's womb. That doesn't make sense."

The father sneers.

"That's the point, genius. Your idiot brother killed three of my sons. I was simply returning the favor."

Bones squats in front of him and stares into his eyes, and I can feel the anger radiating from my brother.

"Instead of going after the man that killed your adult sons, that were just as cruel as you are, you chose to go after an innocent, defenseless child?"

"An eye for an eye," Giovanni growls.

We all know that is not an eye for an eye. Going after Reaper would have been, but he knew damn well he'd never kill my brother. Instead, he went after what matters the most to him. It's cowardly to go after a woman and child, instead of handling things the way a man should.

Bones' lips turn into an evil grin. If he weren't my brother, I'd be worried by it.

"Now you get to watch your remaining sons die."

"I didn't touch her," Edoardo yells out, trying to save his own skin.

This is the problem with families like this. They are fucking weak. Whether I had a hand in something or not, I'd gladly stand by my brothers and die, before trying to save myself. We die together if it comes down to it.

"Kage. Slit their throats. Start with Edoardo."

I pull my knife out as Bones grabs Giovanni's dark hair and yanks his head back.

"Watch your boy die."

Stepping closer, I grab Edoardo's face and push his head back as he whimpers, "Papa," repeatedly and, with one clean swipe of his throat, I end his life. His body falls backward against the cement with a loud thud, as blood squirts from his gaping flesh.

Giovanni trembles while he sobs.

"My son, my son."

Bones glances over to me with a nod.

"Rocco's turn."

I glare at him as I move closer.

"You raped my sister."

He rolls his eyes at me before speaking nonsense.

"She isn't your sister."

While it's true Reaper and Bella aren't married yet, it doesn't matter. The moment my brother told us she was his, she became one of us.

I grab his face the way I did his brother's and slash his throat, as Giovanni screams his name, until his body falls on top of his brother's.

As I chuckle, Bones growls at me.

"What's so fucking funny?"

I point to Psycho as he walks in the door, because this is definitely more his interest than mine. My oldest brother enjoys cutting flesh, almost to a disturbing degree. For me, it's a means to an end. A quick kill. For him, it's intoxicating.

Wiping my knife off on my pants, I put it back in my pocket, because I'm pretty sure the next kill will be Psycho's.

"Any problems?" Bones asks.

Psycho shakes his head.

"Of course not. I have our six best men with Athena. They will not take their eyes off her. And she has been instructed to call you after they get to the hospital."

Bones sighs a relieved breath and says, "Thank you."

"Psycho. Aldo needs to die quickly, so we can clear the house and get to the hospital."

My brother rolls his eyes, and I'd bet money it's because he doesn't like quick. If he had his way, he'd torture Aldo for weeks, at least.

Giovanni whimpers, "There's nobody in the house. We're out here."

All three of us exchange curious glances, and Psycho moves to Aldo, standing over him with a menacing expression.

"Is this true? We can do this the easy way if you're honest, but if I think you're lying, this is going to get rather bloody."

He shakes his head, as he stares at my brother like there's any chance of his life being spared. As he speaks, he looks like he has hope, and he shouldn't.

"There's some staff in the house. The maid, the chef."

"No family?" Psycho asks.

He nods. "My mother and sister, but they were not part of this."

Psycho digs his knife into his stomach, causing him to scream in pain.

"How unfortunate. If they have Abruzzo blood, they are guilty as fucking sin."

He pulls the blade out and Aldo falls back, sobbing endlessly, as Psycho climbs over him and slashes his throat.

# Chapter Seven
## RAINA

I sit as still as possible, but I hear the feet come closer. With every step, I tremble more, hitting my stash of body wash beside me. Instead of being perfectly quiet, the bottle falling over gives me away. The curtain is wrenched back, and my eyes pop open and travel up a large body. He stares at me with amusement.

"Boo," he says with a wicked grin.

He motions with his finger.

"Come out here."

I shake my head.

"If you are here to kill me, just get it done with."

With a smirk, he says, "Your mother and father are in the bedroom, also waiting to die. I want you all together."

Immediately, I get out of my spot, and hit my head while standing up, but ignore it.

"Don't hurt them. Kill me and let them be."

He rubs the side of his clean shaven face with the barrel of his gun.

"You'd die for him? A rapist? A baby killer?"

Shaking my head, I admit the truth.

"No, but for my mother, I would."

He takes my hair between his fingers, and stares at me like he's fascinated.

"Hair as red as fire. Eyes as green as emeralds. You will look stunning in my cage."

"Your what?" I gasp.

"My cage," he says, confirming that I did indeed hear him correctly.

I jerk out of his hold.

"I don't think so. You can kill me. I'm not going to be your fucking pet."

He chuckles obnoxiously.

"Pretty little Firecracker. You will be my *fucking* pet, and anything else I want you to be."

The way he growls 'fucking' makes my skin crawl. And I know, for a fact, I'd rather be dead than to be his anything.

I fold my arms across my chest, letting him know I'm not going along with whatever his sick plan is.

"Anything I do is my choice. You can kill me, but you can't force me to do anything I don't want to."

He grins in response.

"I'm all about choice, Firecracker. I'm going to give you the chance to choose which of your parents lives."

I nearly collapse with relief, but manage to contain it.

"My mother. Let her live. I don't care what you do with my father, but please don't hurt her."

He takes my hand, and pulls me out of the bathroom to the bedroom, where my mother and father kneel, with two other large men standing over them.

The scary man holds his gun up, and places it in my hand, as I stare at him with confusion.

"You kill either your mother or father. You decide which one of them lives."

"What?" I squeak.

"You heard me, Firecracker."

One of the men glares at him.

"What are you doing, Kage?"

"Keeping her. And I suppose, if she chooses, her mother."

So his name is Kage, and he wants to keep me *in* a cage. That can't be a coincidence.

He growls in my ear.

"Choose, Firecracker, before I make the choice for you. I promise you won't like what I decide for you."

Holding the weapon in both of my hands, I slowly lift it in the direction of my father. I don't want to kill him, because I don't want to take anyone's life, but if it's between him and my mother, the choice is obvious.

The other two men step out of the way, as my father stares at me, with an expression that asks me to spare his life, as if I could. I don't really have a choice.

"What makes you think I won't turn and kill you instead?"

The man they call Cage chuckles softly.

"You'd be dead before you pulled the trigger, and then your mother would die a painful death."

Raising the gun, I aim at my father's forehead, hoping to make this quick. My dominant hand trembles slightly, but I steady myself.

I pull the trigger once, and fall backwards because the kickback is strong. I'm not even sure which is louder, the sound of the gun, or my mother's deafening screams. She'll never forgive me for this.

I sit on the floor with the gun in front of me, and stare at my mother on her knees, hands on her face, as she sobs 'Gio' repeatedly. Every time she cries his name, it feels like a knife in my chest. Not for him, but for her. My mother has been a mafia wife since she was eighteen, and essentially sold to him. She doesn't know a world outside of him. He may not have loved her, but I think she loved him. And not only did I kill him, but I did it in front of her.

Reaching down, Cage takes the gun and tucks it into a holster under his jacket, before pulling me to my feet.

"We have to go. Our men will take your mother to my house. If you behave, you'll see her later."

"What?" I ask, as two men come in and take my sobbing mother out of the room.

"No. I did what you wanted. Don't let them hurt her."

He rolls his eyes at me like I'm an idiot.

"Nobody is going to hurt her. She'll be fed, clothed, and will have everything she needs. I guarantee you, she'll be treated far better than your father treated Bella."

*Bella, the blonde girl.*

"Is she okay?"

He turns to me and narrows his gaze.

"You knew she was here, what they were doing, and you did nothing."

The way he says it is like I'm a bitch who didn't care, but does he think I had a choice?

"What was I supposed to do? Save her? Do you know what would have happened, Cage? I would've been killed, and then they would have continued doing what they wanted to her."

He tightens his hold on my wrist, and pulls me out of the room and down the stairs.

"We have to get to the hospital. If she doesn't live, my brother will go on a murderous spree no one in this state is prepared for."

I'm taken to a Range Rover, and he points to the back door.

"Get in."

I stare at him in disbelief, as the other men take off in two different SUVs. If it's just us going in this one, I don't understand why I have to sit in the back.

"I'm not getting in the back."

# Chapter Eight

## KAGE

"What's the problem, Firecracker?"

She folds her arms over her chest, like a defiant little brat that needs to be punished.

"I'm not getting in the back."

I could easily make her sit wherever the fuck I want her to, but I'm intrigued.

"You want to be closer to me? Is that it? Maybe you want to ride my cock while I drive?"

She makes a face, and scrunches up her nose like she smells rotten garbage.

"Don't be gross. Of course I don't."

I run my fingers down her cheek while I laugh.

"Gross? Many women would beg to ride my cock, Firecracker."

Tracing my finger over her bottom lip, I enjoy the softness against my calloused finger. She opens her mouth and bites down, and I quickly retract my hand.

"You want to act like a rabid dog, you'll be treated like one. Remember, this was your doing."

Opening the front door, I growl, "Get in."

She does as she's told, and I take a minute to take her in. Long red hair done in soft curls, dramatic eye makeup complementing the black leather pants, and matching shirt with a plunging neckline.

"You're quite beautiful to look at. It's really too bad you're such a brat."

"Why is that?" She asks as I shut the door. Walking around the suv, I get into the driver's seat and begin to drive.

"Your name is Cage?" she asks, while nervously looking out the window. She digs her nails into her wrists, and I wonder what that's about, assuming it's an anxious habit, so I let it go because she has every reason to have anxiety.

"Yeah."

With wide eyes, she turns her gaze on me.

"Because that's your thing, right? You keep women in cages?"

I shrug.

"It's not always women, but yes."

"Your fingers have a K instead of a C."

I chuckle as I glance at the tattoos on my fingers. Each of my fingers on my right hand have a skull tattoo, with a letter of my name.

"I spell it with a K."

She giggles, and fuck me if it doesn't cause my cock to stir. It's the sweetest sound I think I've heard, and it only makes me wonder what she sounds like when she comes.

"With a K? Like a Kardashian?"

I glare at her as I turn off the highway.

"No. With a K like the fucking letter K."

I pull into the hospital parking lot, and she's still laughing, like she's in on the fucking joke that I'm an idiot. After putting the car in park, I reach up and wrap my hand around her throat, causing her giggles to die in her throat.

I squeeze, cutting her air supply slightly, and her eyes widen as the panic sets in.

"The plan was to kill you. That was my brother's instructions. I suggest you tread carefully, Firecracker. I enjoy looking at you, but that will only take you so far. I think killing you will be far easier than dealing with your attitude."

Her bottom lip trembles as I ease up on my grip.

"We are going to go into the hospital, and check on my brother, his girl, and their baby. You will behave. After all, it is your family that put her in this condition."

46

I release my hand, and am captivated by the red handprint I left on her fair skin. It makes me want to strip her naked, and leave marks everywhere. She rubs at her irritated flesh and snaps me out of my fantasy.

"I'll behave. I promise."

I only half believe her, because I'm not sure this girl has an obedient bone in her body. Is she even capable of it? I guess we'll find out. If I have to kill her right here in this hospital, I will.

"You mean nothing to me. It will not be a challenge to end your life."

"I mean nothing to anybody," she says, so quietly I'm certain I wasn't supposed to hear it, but I did. It makes me curious about her life. I don't really care, just pure curiosity.

After getting out of the vehicle, I walk around to her side and help her out. I wrap my arm around her waist, setting my fingers on the small amount of skin showing between the hem of her shirt and pants. It irritates me that I like the way her warm flesh feels against mine, but I ignore it.

I check my text from Bones, looking for Bella's room number.

**Bones:** *She's in room number 408, but you may want to drop your package off before you come to the hospital. Reaper isn't doing well.*

**Me:** *I'm on my way in with my 'package'.*

I chuckle to myself, because I'm guessing Athena is close by, and he doesn't want her to know that I have my pretty little firecracker against her will. It probably wouldn't surprise her, but she wouldn't agree with it either.

"I could just run."

I tilt my head at her and smirk.

"Yeah?"

47

She shrugs her shoulders and says, "You know who my father is, but you don't even know my name. Fun fact, it's not Firecracker. Maybe I'll dye my hair black, and you'll never find me."

I chuckle as I lean down and inhale the scent of her throat. Fucking magnificent.

"Raina Abruzzo. Age twenty-two. The youngest of the children. You have dreams of making it as a fashion designer, and wish to move far away from your family. I know everything I need to know, Firecracker, so fucking behave."

She swallows hard, and I grab her arm tightly and drag her into the hospital with me. For a brief moment, she keeps her mouth closed, but unfortunately, it doesn't last long. We step into the elevator and I press number four. The second the doors close, she runs her mouth again.

"I'm not like the women you're probably used to. I'll bite you. I'll fucking stab you if I get the chance. You won't be keeping me in a cage, because I'm not a dog. You'd do yourself a big favor by letting me go."

Wrapping my hand around her throat, I push her against the wall of the elevator, and put my face an inch from hers. So close I can feel her heavy breaths on my skin. I ignore the way my cock pushes against my zipper.

"You are different. I've never had a mafia princess in my cage. I can't wait to watch you grab onto the bars and cry for me. Seeing you drop to your knees and beg for me will be my greatest joy. You're right, you're not a dog, but fuck, Firecracker, you'll look so goddamn beautiful crawling like one on a leash."

She parts her lips and bites down on my bottom lip, causing me to groan, not with pain but pleasure. I had no intention of fucking her, but she's making me want to. My eyes drop to my blood, coating her lips, and it's stunning. I grab a fistful of her hair and pull hard, as I slam my lips to hers. Her anger is palpable, even though she kisses me back. She hates me, and I fucking hate her too. Even so, I can't wait to shove my cock into her throat.

# Chapter Nine

## RAINA

I kissed my captor. Who the hell does that? Kage being hot shouldn't matter. I should've bitten his lip harder.

With a grin on his face, like he's won some kind of stupid game, he yanks me into the hospital room where the blonde woman lays sobbing, with a man beside her. He turns, and stares at me with a death glare, when his brother says my name. The recognition is instant, as he charges for me, grabs my throat with both hands, and squeezes. It's different from when Kage had his hands on me.

His eyes stare into mine, and are dark as coal. His intention is clear, but his words are even more so.

"My baby is dead. Your family killed my child, and now I'll kill theirs."

"Reaper!" I hear Kage's voice in the distance, but I can't see him, or anything, as my vision gets blurry.

"She didn't hurt Bella. Take your fucking hands off her, brother."

It isn't Kage that gets him to release me. It's his woman, when she says what must be his real name.

"Nico! Don't. Let her go."

He removes his hands from my neck and I fall to my knees, coughing, when Kage lifts me into his arms, and places me on the couch in the fancy room.

This is not an average hospital room. It's a large suite with two bathrooms. There's one off to the side across from the bed, and another all the way across the room, that I assume is for guests of the patient. It has a large light blue sectional, and two sitting chairs. The Bonetti men stand as if they're ready for a fight to break out at a moment's notice. Large muscular men, wide stances, threatening scowls. Each of them only seems more intense than the last.

Kage runs his fingers over my throat, inspecting what are probably red handprints from his brother. I've always been warned that the Bonetti brothers are monsters, and now I'm beginning to believe the warning was genuine.

Two other men walk back into the room, and I instantly remember them from my house.

"Where the fuck were you?"

One holds up a cup of coffee.

"Are you going to introduce me to your pretty little pet?"

I roll my eyes as Kage says, "Psycho, this is Raina. Raina, Psycho."

He nods and then looks back at his brother.

"Remember our pact? I'm not kidding, I will fucking stab you."

"Will? Why wait? There's no time like the present," I say quietly, but Kage hears me and flashes me a glare.

"I don't think I should be here," I whisper, as I watch the angry one, who I now know is Reaper Bonetti, with his woman.

Tears run down his face as he apologizes to her repeatedly.

"I'm sorry. I did this."

She wraps her arms around his neck.

"No, Nico. This is not your doing."

If they weren't Bonettis it would be beautiful, the way they comfort each other. As if the other's pain means more than their own.

Kage points everybody out to me, but keeps his voice low.

"That's Bones. He's the head of the family. And that's his wife, Athena. Reaper, you kind of met, and his girl, Bella."

I have never met any of them, but the names I've heard before. One more than the others.

"Reaper. He killed my brothers."

I know why he feels guilty because, honestly, he started this. It's not that I think she deserved what was done to her. The men in my family are repulsive. There's a lot of criminal activity in the mafia world, but my family takes it to an entirely different degree. Any other family would've gone after the man that did this to them. Mine went after a woman, and brutally raped her, before killing her unborn child. Of course, they're all dead now, so it makes sense to me why he wanted to kill me, and probably my mother too.

"When can I see my mom?"

"As soon as you earn the right to a visit."

I sit up on the couch and run a hand through my hair.

"Is she in a cage?"

He shakes his head and sits beside me.

"No. She is in a room with a private bathroom, small kitchen, and a television."

My eyes snap to his angrily.

"And yet you intend to keep me in a cage?"

He grins at me with an evil smirk.

"Yes, Firecracker. You mesmerize me, and your mother does not."

"Is there a way to un-mesmerize you, because I think I prefer that?"

He chuckles loudly and says, "That's not a word, Firecracker. Looks like somebody is getting a dictionary for her birthday."

I roll my eyes at him because at this point I doubt I'll be alive for my birthday.

"Some sort of a blunt object is at the top of my wish list. Or a gun."

His brother, Psycho, taps on his shoulder, and Kage turns away from me and talks to him quietly, so he thinks I can't hear him, but I can.

"No, this is nothing like Bones or Reaper. I know our pact, and trust me, it's not happening. I'm not falling for disgusting Abruzzo filth. I'm going to cage her and then kill her. I promise you, I'm not keeping her."

Kage walks over to his other brother, Reaper, and they all talk amongst themselves, and this time I can't hear a word, but I'm not really trying to. I'm still attempting to process his words to Psycho. I don't like him any more than he likes me, but it still stings to have anyone call you disgusting. Even when you consider the source, it's painful.

Every once in a while I see one of them look at me, and I know I'm the topic of conversation.

Kage walks over to me.

"Come on, Princess. Time to go home."

I swallow down the bile in my throat from that one word, and dig my nails into my wrist, and Kage growls at me.

"Fucking stop that."

He grabs my hand and pulls me off the couch, but I jerk back from him.

"Wait."

I glance between Bella and Reaper, his face radiates pure anguish, and it makes me hate my family even more for what they've done.

"Can I talk to her?"

Reaper answers for everyone.

"No. Get out."

Bella speaks up.

"Nico, stop. She can talk."

I step closer to the bed, but keep a distance, so they don't think I mean her any harm.

"I'm really sorry for what they did to you. I never could've prevented it. They would've killed me, and carried on with their plans. I never wanted this. I certainly didn't want any harm to come to your baby. My father felt justified, because Reaper killed his three sons. I didn't agree, but I'm only a woman. For the record, I did make it clear to them how wrong it was, but I couldn't stop it. I know you all hate me and want me dead, and I don't blame you.

Soon enough, you'll get your wish, and I don't want to go to the grave without you knowing the truth. I'm so sorry."

Reaper growls through a clenched jaw.

"Kage, get her out of here. Now."

He moves quickly, scooping me into his arms, and races out of the room.

# Chapter Ten
## KAGE

"What the hell?" she complains as she puts her arms around my neck to prevent herself from falling.

I narrow my gaze at her.

"He will kill you."

She glances away from me, as I step into the elevator and set her on her feet.

"You will anyway, so why does it matter? Surely you don't want to keep someone so disgusting alive longer than you have to."

Raina was not meant to hear that conversation. It wasn't malicious, and hurting her wasn't intentional, but it was the truth. My brothers have no problem with me having a little fun with her before I kill her. Bones doesn't comment on our sex lives, but getting involved with an Abruzzo would never be tolerated. It doesn't matter anyway, because I'm not the guy that settles down. I don't do feelings, I'm honestly not sure I'm capable of it. Bones has told me, more than once, that Psycho and I were born without hearts. He might be right.

If I'm honest with myself though, I've never seen a woman more beautiful than Raina. She's the kind of stunning you never get tired of looking at. If she weren't an Abruzzo, I'd let her live for that reason alone. But she is an Abruzzo. It's not a choice. She'll have to die. If I don't do it, one of my brothers will.

"You're an Abruzzo. The entire line must die, yourself included. We're just taking a slight detour."

She trembles as a tear rolls down her cheek and, fuck, it just makes her more alluring. The woman I should have already killed. Her tight little body calls to me like a siren's song. My little firecracker is pure temptation. I'm like a dehydrated man staring at a cup of poison. He knows he'll die if he drinks from the cup, but he can't control himself. I already know she's my end and beginning. My destruction and salvation. I know I should never fuck her.

*Should.*

Yet, it's exactly what I'm going to do. Not because I want to, but because I have to. I'm drawn to her fire, knowing it'll burn. I should pull myself from the flames before it's too late. There's that word again.

*Should.*

Knowing the right thing to do, and doing it, are two different things.

I'll fuck her for a few days, and by then I'll be bored anyway and kill her. That way, everyone gets what they need.

*Except her.*

I shrug off the thought, because what she needs doesn't matter. She's an Abruzzo.

Grabbing her arm, I pull her out of the open elevator, and yank her through the hallway of the hospital.

"Would you fucking stop?"

She falls for the third time today, and I growl at her.

"Let's go."

"I hate you," she bites, as I yank her off the floor.

Once we make it outside, I hoist her over my shoulder while she kicks my stomach. I open the door to my black Range Rover, and toss her in the backseat where she belongs, before getting into the front seat. I lock the doors so she can't get any bright ideas, and glance in the mirror at her staring death glares at me. She looks like a wild animal. Wide eyes, her red hair a matted glorious mess.

I adjust myself as I drive, and she scowls at me.

"You're disgusting."

I smirk at her.

"I guess we have something in common, Firecracker."

She kicks at my seat repeatedly, and doesn't stop until I'm thoroughly annoyed.

"Take a look behind you."

Raina tries to refuse to look, but curiosity gets the better of her, and she turns and spots the cage in the back.

"That's right, Firecracker. Keep it up and that's how you'll be traveling."

She turns back around, and sits still with her hands on her lap, as she says something so quiet I barely hear her.

"I must have been a terrible person in my previous life, and I'm paying for it now. After what has been done to me in this one, nothing should faze me. This shouldn't hurt like it does."

I don't respond, but I do wonder what's been done to her. My information on Raina is limited, even though I made it sound to her like I know every deep, dark secret she holds. The only thing I know about her, other than what I told her, is that her father has been actively trying to sell her to another family for four years, since her eighteenth birthday. Arranged marriages are not uncommon in our world, although it's something my family doesn't do. My mother put a squash to that when we were little. She didn't argue with my father about much, but for that she did. It was important to her that her children marry for love, not power. My father agreed, because if you run your business well, you don't need to sell off your daughters like fucking livestock to survive. Weak men run businesses that don't profit. And I've never seen a mafia family as chaotic as the Abruzzos. And desperate.

I have no doubt my pretty little firecracker has been through the ringer. She'll probably be relieved to die.

Glancing back before I turn into my circular driveway, I spot her brushing a tear away. She's beautiful. A mixture of vulnerability, and brat. I always thought I liked submissive women that do as they're told, but I like her venomous bite.

59

I park and immediately open the back door and pull her out of the SUV.

Her gaze is dark, and I spot something I've never seen before. Raina's light is covered with a dark shadow, and I instantly recognize the pain bubbling just under the surface before my little snake coils up and strikes.

She headbutts me, causing immediate blinding pain. I can't see a damn thing, but as she turns to run, I grab her throat and pin her against the vehicle. Making the mistake of getting too close to her, she bites my lip until it bleeds. Again. I run my tongue over the pool of blood on my bottom lip and grin at her.

"Bad pet. You'll pay for that."

Winding her hair around my fist, I yank her to my front door, while she screams beautiful obscenities at me.

# Chapter Eleven
## RAINA

He pulls me by my hair, through the house, and up the stairs. The more I struggle, the harder his grip, so I stop fighting him. I'm not stupid. I know there's only one way this ends. Kage takes me into a bedroom, and I take a quick glance around. It's a standard bedroom, other than the size. It's massive, with a King-sized bed on one side, with black satin sheets that make me roll my eyes. How cliché. All of the furniture is black. The end table, armoire, dresser. There is no color to the room. And then I gulp. There's a gold cage in one corner. It's not like anything I've ever seen before. The thick gold bars are built into the ceiling and run all the way to the floor. It appears to have been handmade, with three small skulls on each bar. I stand immobile when he comes up behind me, putting something around my neck, as he murmurs beside my ear.

"This necklace should help you remember to behave."

Metal pokes into my throat, and I know it's not a necklace.

"What the fuck is this?"

He chuckles softly against my skin, causing shivers to run down my spine.

"I told you, if you act like a rabid dog, you'll be treated like one."

"They put rabid dogs down," I hiss through clenched teeth.

Kage goes over to the chair in the corner, takes a seat, and holds up a controller.

"Do as you're told, and I will not use this. If you're disobedient, you'll be shocked."

I fold my arms over my chest.

"You are not going to fucking shock me. That's ridiculous."

He arches an eyebrow at me and continues his insanity.

"Take your clothes off, Raina. No bra, but you can keep your panties on."

Again, he holds up the controller, to remind me what he'll do to me. I wonder, will he really? Only a monster would treat a human like this. Maybe he will, but I'm betting he won't follow through on it.

I shake my head in refusal.

"I'm not taking anything off."

He's obviously hard, as he adjusts himself.

"Oh, Principessa. Is that what they call you? Pretty little princess used to having her way. This is your final warning."

I see red, because only one man has ever called me that.

"Don't call me that, ever again. I'll do what you want, but don't fucking call me that."

His face shows surprise, before he quickly hides it away, with the sexy as hell clenching of his jaw. I hate it. I hate him.

"Alright, Firecracker. Have it your way. Now, do as you were told."

I remove my shirt as he watches me, leaning back in his chair, legs spread like a fucking king on his throne. His gaze follows my every movement, with a heat so intense I can nearly feel his touch on my skin. I want to hate it so bad it hurts. There should be no part of me that likes the way he's staring at me. But I do. I'm trapped in his gaze, as he stares at me like I'm something special. Nobody has ever done that. Knowing what he plans to do to me ends that feeling quickly.

"Take off your bra." He groans as he squeezes his length.

Reaching behind my back, I unfasten the snaps and slide it down my arms, until it drops to the floor.

I remove my pants, and place them on the floor, and watch him as he removes his shirt, never taking his eyes from me. His chest and arms are like a work of art. There's so much ink, and part of me wants to trace my fingers over it. Yet, another part of me wants to put this collar on him, and shock him until he breathes his final breath.

"Crawl to me."

I gasp, because he's taking this dog fantasy of his to a crazy level.

"Kage. Seriously."

He holds up the controller.

"Seriously."

I drop to my knees, because I don't want to be shocked.

"I'm running out of patience," he says, in a low voice that speaks to my core.

I crawl to him, slowly with trepidation, as he watches me like I'm the most fascinating thing he has ever seen.

He tangles his fingers in my hair as he continues his perusal, like I'm something bizarre he has never seen before.

"Beg me to fuck you."

I tilt my head back, meeting his gaze, and speak with a shaky voice that tells him how I feel.

"Even if I don't want that?"

He smirks at me. "And what do you want, little Firecracker?"

I roll my eyes at him and tell him the truth.

"First, I want to wrap this fucking collar around your dick, and shock you so many times you can never get it up again. More than that, though, I want you to die, so I can live."

He chuckles softly, as if what I said is actually funny.

"I love it when you talk dirty to me, baby."

Motioning for me to come to him, he says, "Come up here, Firecracker."

Kage pats his leg, and I shake my head no.

"I don't want to shock myself accidentally."

Placing the remote on the small table beside the chair, he grins at me.

"Better?"

I breathe a sigh of relief, and climb onto his lap, like the fucking dog he apparently thinks I am.

"If you're a good girl for me, maybe I'll remove the collar for a little while. Would that make you happy?"

I close my eyes as a tear slides down my cheek. It's not stripping naked for him that hurts. Not even being forced to crawl to him. It's the inhumane treatment. The shock collar causes terror unlike any other. He knows this, I'm sure of it. It's why he's doing it.

"Yes."

A whimper escapes from me as he brushes a thumb over my nipple.

"Are you ready to beg for me?"

He can shock me until I'm dead, there is zero chance of me begging him to brutally rip my virginity from me. And he would be brutal, I have no doubt.

"No, because I don't want to have sex with you, Kage. I'm a virgin, and I want to keep it that way."

His eyes darken immediately, as he runs his tongue over his bottom lip. If I thought that would make him stop this, I was wrong.

"My brother has a theory about virgins. He thinks if you fuck one, you never get over them. Like a virgin pussy is magical, and changes a man. I guess we'll find out."

I try to use his words to my advantage, because I am quickly running out of options.

"If that's true, it could spell trouble for you. It might be better to not tempt fate."

He presses his hand against my face, and I hate how gentle he appears at this moment, because I know enough about Kage to know he's anything but soft. I can feel his hard length under me, and it feels so big. I hope I'm wrong, because I think he might break me.

He grins at me, appearing pleased with himself.

"Yes, pretty little Firecracker, I'm going to break you. Before this is over, you will be a ruined mess."

My cheeks flush pink, as I realize I spoke out loud, which was not my intention.

He reaches both of his hands behind me and removes the shock collar.

"This is temporary, Raina. Do not mistake my kindness for weakness. If you choose disobedience, this will go back on in a flash. Do you understand?"

"Yes," I breathe.

There are no words to convey the relief that floods my system. After all that I've been through, it's strange that the stupid pink collar felt like the worst. I'm sure it's not, but it felt that way. Maybe because I wasn't being treated like a human, or because of the constant threat of pain. I don't know, but I didn't like it.

"Thank you."

# Chapter Twelve

## KAGE

"I'll take my chances."

My voice comes out deep and low, probably telling her how badly I want to be inside her. Using her hair as reins, I pull her closer and swipe my tongue across her lips. She places her small hands on my chest, as I press my lips to hers and kiss her slowly. Raina whimpers sweetly as I push my tongue into her mouth. The scent of roses invades my senses, and it's all her.

I grab onto her hips, rise from my chair, carry her to the bed, and lie her down. She trembles as she stares at me, wide eyed. If there was a place for her to run to, she'd be on her feet.

Placing my hand on her throat, her pulse beats against my palm as I remind her.

"Don't make me put it back on."

She squeezes her eyes shut tight as she whispers, "I won't."

I've never understood my youngest brother's obsession with eyes, but I do right now. Raina's green ones stir something inside me, and it pisses me off that she has taken them from me.

"Eyes on me."

Immediately, her gaze is on me again, and I hook my thumbs into the sides of her panties and pull them down slowly, like I'm unwrapping a gift I've waited forever for.

I've never fucked a virgin, so I don't know if this fear is normal, but she's fucking terrified, as she shakes like a leaf.

"I'm going to make you feel good first."

Her bottom lip trembles as she talks.

"If, for whatever reason you don't kill me, and I return to my family without my virginity intact, I'm dead. By taking this from me, you're sealing my fate."

I look at her with a shocked expression.

"Your father is dead, Raina."

A tear rolls down her cheek.

"Did you really think you could wipe out the entire family in one house? I promise you, my uncle will be waiting to take over where my dad left off. And he will not think twice about killing me."

Something in my chest twists, and I'm tempted to tell her everything will be okay, but that would be a lie. For her, everything will not be okay, so I give her a softer version of the truth.

"I won't let him get close enough to hurt you. You're mine now, and only I decide if you live or die. Now spread your legs, and show me the pretty pussy I'm going to devour."

I strip out of my pants, climb on the bed between her legs, and stare in fucking awe. She's fucking stunning, from those beautiful green eyes, to her pebbled nipples, tiny waist, and that pussy that makes my mouth water. She's absolutely breathtaking. I've seen my share of naked women, but never one like this. It's as if she was crafted from my goddamn fantasies.

Pushing her legs back, I lower myself, and inhale the scent of her pussy.

"Fuck. You smell so good, little Firecracker."

I slide my tongue along her slit, and she whimpers loudly, causing my dick to get harder. Flicking my tongue over her clit causes an immediate reaction from her, as she lifts her hips and lets out these breathy moans that I'll never forget. Fucking perfection.

"You taste like the sweetest honey I've ever had," I say, as I dip my tongue inside her, lapping up my new favorite flavor.

I place my lips around her swollen clit and suck. Gently at first, then harder, as she reacts by clawing her nails into my shoulders, and she cries out in ecstasy. She's close to an orgasm, but she stops me.

"What's your real name?"

I glance up at her, my face covered in her wetness, as I arch an eyebrow.

"Why?"

Her eyes dart to the cage in the corner of the room while she answers me.

"Kage makes me think of captivity. It's not very sexy."

"Lorenzo," I answer, as I go back to my meal.

Going down on a woman has always been a means to an end. Make them wet and get what I want. Yeah, I'm a selfish asshole that way, but as she reaches her climax, and claws at me like a fucking feral animal, I know I want to watch this again.

"Lorenzo," she screams out, as her body trembles for me.

*My name on her tongue, her taste in my mouth, her gorgeous body in my bed.*

It's all fucking intoxicating.

As I prepare to ruin her, I wonder if I'm also organizing my own end.

Killing her isn't optional. If I don't, Bones will. There is no scenario where my brothers will let her live. I'll fuck her a few times, and get her out of my system. It won't be a problem. I am not Bones or Reaper. I don't get attached, but I'll never forget this taste.

Climbing over her, I pin her legs back and push into her. I only make it an inch, when I can't go further, and she screams in pain.

I rub her clit to distract her, and she moans through her tears.

"Relax for me. It'll hurt less."

The frustration shows on her face, and I have to bite my lip to not chuckle.

"Just fuck me, Lorenzo. If you're going to do it, do it. If you're not, then get off me."

I arch an eyebrow while I stare at her.

"You are such a fucking brat. That mouth of yours is going to get you in an awful lot of trouble."

Grabbing the backs of her thighs, I pull out and push back into her, all the way, as she screams at me.

"Fuck!" she yells at the top of her lungs.

I'm an asshole, but I don't enjoy a woman not feeling good. Her getting off is as important as my orgasm. I want to just fuck her, but I hold myself back because I need her to come again.

I move over top of her, and support myself with one hand on the mattress beside her head, and keep my other one free to touch her fantastic tits.

She reaches her hands up, then yanks them back like she stuck them into a fire.

"Touch me, Firecracker."

Her trembling hands land on my chest and, as I look at her, I know, if I had a choice, I wouldn't end her life. She's too beautiful to die. Raina's crime was being born into the wrong family. It's not fair, but it is what it is. Any Abruzzo living, while Reaper's child is dead, will never be acceptable. For him, her living would be a cruel form of torture. For now, I'll enjoy her sinful body.

Pulling my hips back, I immediately snap forward, until I'm buried to the hilt in her sweet pussy. I do the same thing over and over again, forcing myself to hold back on my orgasm until she comes. I'm trying to do the right thing, and then she places her hand on the side of my face and whispers softly.

"Lorenzo, please let me live. Don't punish me for my family's crimes."

I don't respond, I just pick up my pace and fuck her like she's nothing but a fucktoy, because that is all Raina can ever be to me.

My orgasm crawls up the base of my spine as my abs tighten, and I groan softly as I release inside her, filling her with my cum.

I get off her in an instant.

"Go use the bathroom while you can."

She looks shell-shocked, and maybe a little surprised that I didn't let her come first.

"Now, Raina."

I run a hand through my hair, as she scrambles off the bed and uses the bathroom. When she comes out, she tries to hide her body, as if she could.

"Get in the cage."

She lowers her head before shaking it.

"Just when I think you can't disappoint me more than you already do, *Kage,* you prove me wrong."

There's a bite when she says my name, but I ignore it as she moves to the cage. I lock her in, and look down at her sad eyes. Not just sad, but filled with devastation.

"I'll be back later."

She sits in the corner of the cage with her knees up, arms around her legs, as tears fall from her eyes. I know this is not what every girl dreams of happening after losing her virginity, but I'm not a hero. I can't save her from my own damn family. I can't save her from me.

# Chapter Thirteen
## KAGE

I'm fucked. Absolutely fucked. Looking into her eyes, as she all but begged me to let her live, fucking did things to me. She asked me to not punish her for her family's crimes, and fuck me, Raina's right. She should not die because those assholes raped a woman, and killed a baby. How the hell am I supposed to look at Reaper, and tell him two members of their family will live? The plan was for all of them to die. No more Abruzzos. The entire line would be wiped out. Bones is the head of the family, and he'll be the first to tell me she has to die. We don't always kill every member of a family when we have problems, but this is not your normal problem. Going against my family would have tragic outcomes for me. I could lose everything that has ever mattered to me.

I don't care about many things. My family is all I have. Like anybody else, I have friends, but they don't matter to me the way my brothers do. I would gladly take a bullet for any of them. My mind is racing as I get into my car and start driving. I need advice, but my options are limited. Obviously, I can't talk to Reaper or Bones about this. And honestly, Psycho will probably stab me, thinking I'm in love with her. I'm not. I barely fucking know her. It's not about that.

I text a buddy of mine while I'm driving. Yes, I know it's dangerous, but I do a lot of fucking things that are dangerous.

**Me:** *Hey, man. I need to talk through some family bullshit. Are you busy?*

**Dante:** *Nope. I'm having a drink with my brother.*

**Me:** *Where?*

**Dante:** *The Devil. Where else?*

**Me:** *On my way.*

I pull up to The Devil, Domenic De Luca's club, and park in a spot designated for the De Lucas as I snicker to myself. This is how the entire war with the Abruzzos escalated. My brother, Reaper, killed one of them over a goddamn parking spot. When he told me, I knew shit was going to get out of hand. Retaliation is a guarantee in our world, but my brother doesn't think about shit like that. Before Bella, he didn't have a reason to care. Had the tables been turned, we would've gone after the man that wronged us, not a woman, and an unborn child. We do a lot of shit that most of society would claim to be wrong, and downright evil, but even we have lines we won't cross. The Bonettis aren't like the De Lucas though. We don't have some sort of code that says we won't hurt women. If it needs to be done, it will be, which is why I know for a fact that Raina will die, by my hands or one of my brothers'.

I walk into the club, and head straight to the spiral staircase that leads to Domenic's office, because that's where they always are. After knocking, I enter and spot Domenic behind his desk, and his brother Dante on the black leather sofa, with a drink in his hand.

He sits back and nods at the bottle, and empty glass, on Domenic's desk.

"Grab a drink, brother."

I pour myself nearly a full glass of Whiskey, and they both chuckle.

"Oh, it's one of those situations," Domenic says.

Joining Dante on the sofa, I take a gulp of my drink. The burn in my throat is welcoming, as it travels through me.

Dante turns to me with a knowing grin.

"This is about a woman."

74

I nod slowly as I admit, "We went after the Abruzzos and I took their daughter."

Domenic arches an eyebrow as he leans back in his chair, but doesn't say anything.

"My brothers expect me to kill her, and I should. Her father and brothers brutally raped Bella, Reaper's girl, and killed their unborn baby. Bones ordered us to kill every living Abruzzo. That was the plan."

"And then you fucked her," Domenic says plainly.

I throw back the rest of my drink.

"I did, but it's not about that. She begged me not to kill her. Not to punish her for her family's crimes. And she's right, she shouldn't be killed for the choices of four vile men. Yet, I don't see another option, because I have to follow Bones' orders, and of course, how can I do that to Reaper?"

Dante looks over to me.

"Are you in love with this girl?"

I shake my head no.

"No, you know me. I don't do that love bullshit, and I barely know her anyway."

Domenic laughs, like I told a funny joke.

"My personal opinion is, it's not right to kill the girl. What has she done to wrong you? Nothing. But… Going against your family may cost you. Bones can't just turn a blind eye to such behavior."

And that's the problem. I know he's right.

He continues, and I listen to every word, because I trust both Domenic and Dante with my life.

"Either you kill the girl or go against your family. It's that simple. You could talk to Bones, but if his mind is made up, it won't change anything. So you need to decide for yourself. How important is her life? What are you willing to lose to save it?"

I sigh audibly as Domenic stares into his glass, like he's lost in the past.

"My wife was also from a rival family. You know the story, but I thought I'd kill her as well, and you know we're typically against that. It would have been a mistake to hold her responsible for her father's decisions."

He swallows hard.

"I can't imagine my life without her. I don't want to. I'd gladly take her place, rather than live without Giada."

I get up and pour myself another shot.

"It's not like that, though. I'm not in love with her. I don't want to marry her, or for her to have my goddamn babies. I just don't know if I can kill her."

I sit back down with my drink in my hand, and Dante looks at me pointedly.

"You've never had an issue taking a woman's life before. If you're honest with yourself, I think you'll find there's something there. Maybe not love, but some sort of affection. There's a reason you don't want to kill the girl you had every intention of killing."

Suddenly everything is clear. I don't have feelings for Raina. I'm a fucking Bonetti man. We do not shy away from killing our enemies. Our family comes first. There's no right or wrong.

I rise from the chair and nod to both of them.

"Thank you for the clarity. I know what I'm going to do."

Domenic asks, "Which is?"

I shrug my shoulders.

"I'm going to kill her. An order is an order. This is my family, and I cannot go against my brothers."

As I turn to walk out the door, Dante calls to me.

"Hey, Kage."

Glancing over my shoulder, my eyes snap to him, and he looks at me with sadness.

"You're going to regret it, I promise you. Betraying your family is not something to take lightly but, fuck, if it was Natalia, Drake and I would hide her. Forever if we had to."

76

In my head, I'm screaming 'but you love Nat', because Drake and Dante both do. I don't fucking love Raina. She is nothing to me, other than a pussy to slide into.

# Chapter Fourteen
## RAINA

The cage isn't the punishment he thinks it is. It's giant. I'm not trapped in a small space. I would like a shower, but other than that, it's not terrible. Having Kage take my virginity and, seconds later, walk away? That was far worse than these gold metal bars, although I'm not a fan of the dried cum on the inside of my thighs. I never imagined my first time would be magical. Had my father had his way, it would've been with the husband he forced me to marry. I begged Kage to spare my life and, for some reason I don't understand, it seemed to set him off. He couldn't have been surprised that I'd want to live. Doesn't everybody?

The door opens, and he storms in, appearing to be furious when he looks at me. His eyes are dark as coal, as his body nearly vibrates with anger.

He walks over to the end table, and sets his gun on top of it, before stripping off his clothes. I try not to look, because I don't want to be attracted to him. Kage Bonetti is not a likeable man. He may be better than my father and brothers were, but that doesn't make him good. A lesser evil does not make a righteous man.

"I wanted to spare your life, Firecracker, but I can't."

I don't say anything, because what could I possibly say? His mind is made up, and begging obviously isn't going to change it now.

"I'm going to end your life tonight. Better to get it done with, rather than postponing the inevitable. Any last requests?"

His words steal all the breath from my lungs.

I knew he was going to kill me, but I didn't realize it'd be so soon. There's something odd about knowing your life is going to end. I'm filled with both fear and relief. My life hasn't been easy, and maybe it's better this way. No more Leo. No more nightmares.

"I'd like to have a shower first."

He nods in understanding as he opens the cage.

"Do you want to know, or do you want me to just do it? I'm going to make it as painless as possible."

I turn and stare directly at him.

"I want you to tell me. I want you to look into my eyes. And more than anything, I want you to never forget taking the life of a woman who never did anything to you, or your family. Do what you need to do, Lorenzo, but I hope I fucking haunt you, for the rest of the days of your life."

He opens his mouth but quickly shuts it, and waves his hand toward the bathroom, telling me to take my last shower.

I walk into the bathroom, and turn the water on and, once I get it as hot as I can stand, I step in, while a naked and hard Kage stands in the doorway, watching me.

"Are you going to stand there watching me the entire time? Like a fucking pervert?"

He chuckles softly and says, "I am."

As I attempt to ignore him, I stand under the showerhead mounted directly in the center of the shower. It sprays at the back, at the front, and there's a rainfall showerhead above. At least my last shower is a fancy one, although big enough for ten people. The only thing I'd change about it is the glass doors. I'd prefer a dark curtain, so he couldn't watch me, while stroking himself, like he is. I don't notice the way his cock slides in and out of his fist. I don't notice the way the muscles in his arm flex as he does it. And I definitely don't notice the way his sexy jaw clenches as he stares at me, like I'm more than the girl he's about to kill.

"Goddamn it, Raina," he growls, as he storms over to the shower door and yanks it open furiously. He wraps his hand around my throat, and slams me to the shower wall.

"Why do I want you so much?"

I blink fast as the water comes in all directions. He hits a button, and the water from overhead stops, as he continues to stare at me with a heated expression. This man is going to kill me so I hate myself for noticing the water dripping from his face to his strong chest. I despise that my executioner makes me feel anything at all.

"Spread your legs," he groans. I do and he slams his lips to mine. He pushes his tongue into my mouth, and the butterflies swirl in my stomach. The ones that shouldn't be there. How can the man that's planning to kill me, be the only man that's ever made me feel alive?

Breaking our kiss, he squats down and wraps his arms around my thighs and lifts me, pinning me against the shower wall. He lowers me onto his huge cock with a sexy grunt.

"Fuck, Firecracker. This pussy is perfect."

I wrap my arms around his neck for stability, not because I want him closer. At least that's what I keep telling myself.

Holding onto my ass, he moves me up and down his length, and it doesn't hurt like it did the first time. This time it feels good as he fills me completely. He keeps hitting a spot that makes my toes curl, and forces a moan out of me.

He presses his face into my neck, and inhales with a low groan.

"So fucking beautiful. Why do you need to be like this? You smell so goddamn good, I'm never going to get you out of my head. If it's any consolation, Firecracker, you are going to haunt me. I'll try like fucking hell to forget about you, but I already know, I never will."

Reluctantly, I kiss his neck softly and whisper, "Then don't do it, Lorenzo. This is your choice."

"It's not. Fuck, I wish it was. I don't think you should die because of what they did. I'm sorry. I cannot go against my brothers."

I lay my head on his shoulder while he fucks me like he owns me. And because I'm a sick and twisted person, the knowledge that my life is almost over causes an orgasm to crash in on me, like an unforgiving ocean, dragging me under over and over again.

81

"Lorenzo," I whimper, as I shake against him, and he speaks words of praise I wish he wouldn't.

"So beautiful, Raina. Perfect."

He pulls back and slams forward one last time, filling me completely with his seed, as his cock spasms inside me.

Kissing me softly on the lips, he pulls me off him and sets me down.

"I'll give you a few minutes to yourself, and then we'll go to another room and take care of it."

Kage leaves the shower, and I stand there in disbelief. 'Take care of it' were his words, like we're talking about doing the dishes, or taking the trash out. Some random chore, not the life of a human being. Fighting is useless, because the end result will be the same. I've tried to appeal to his humanity, but maybe he has none.

I understand the fucked up politics of a mafia family, and realize the outcome for him if he doesn't kill me. For me, my life means everything, but for him, it means nothing. An inconvenience. It's not worth what his brother would probably do to him. For my entire life, my existence on this earth has been contingent on mafia men deeming me worthy of breathing. It makes sense that it ends this way. At least now the pain can stop. No more visits from Leo. He will never touch me again, and that's been my biggest dream since I was seven years old.

# Chapter Fifteen
## KAGE

After pulling a pair of sweatpants on, I hear her talking to herself as the water shuts off. It wasn't intentional, but the door was left open, and her words stop me in my tracks.

*At least now the pain can stop. No more visits from Leo. He will never touch me again.*

I may have no choice but to end her life, but if her uncle has been abusing her, he will not only die, but painfully so.

Handing her a t-shirt when she comes out in a towel, she whispers her thanks.

"I'd like to say goodbye to my mother first."

I grab my gun off the end table and glance at her.

"Follow me."

Will she try to get away? There's a chance, but she won't get far. I nod to my security guy stationed outside her mother's door.

"Go take ten. Give her some privacy."

Adelina Abruzzo runs to her daughter, and hugs her tightly.

"I'm sorry," Raina cries.

Her mother glares at me as I stand in the doorway, and whispers something in her ear. I can't hear what the words are, and I don't really try to, because it doesn't matter.

"Lorenzo was kind enough to let me say goodbye, Mama."

Kind enough?

Jesus, she's got to be fucking with my head.

Her mother shakes her head.

"He's not kind. *Figlia*, he's no less of a monster than your father was."

Aside from the fact that I would never do what he and his sons did to Bella, she isn't wrong. There is little thought of doing the right thing in the mafia. We don't have a moral compass. Choices are made based on what's right for the family. Our family comes first, and everything else is secondary.

*Honor.*

*Trust.*

*Loyalty.*

*Respect.*

*Family.*

These are the things we live by. If anything, or anyone, jeopardizes our family, they die. Her family harmed ours, so they can't continue to exist. This didn't start with Reaper killing three of the Abruzzo men. That's just what escalated it. Stealing our men years ago, when my father was in charge, was the very beginning. We still don't know if they took them for information, or if there was another reason. It doesn't matter, because very soon the remaining Abruzzos will be gone.

"It's time, Raina," I say, because I want to get this over with.

She kisses her mother on the cheek.

"Bye, Mama, I love you."

The metal of the gun in the back of my pants presses against my skin. The coolness reminds me of what I'm going to do. Raina follows me to the bedroom and glances at the bed, covered in protective plastic. She's quiet and brave. There's not a tear on her face as she lies on the bed without being instructed.

This is my only chance to get the information I want from her.

"Has Leo been sexually abusing you?"

She closes her eyes and nods her confirmation.

"Since I was seven."

"And these scars on your hip?"

"Self inflicted," she whispers, "but he's the reason."

I swallow hard as I stare at her, shaking slightly on the bed.

"I'm going to make his death excruciating."

She shrugs her shoulders slightly.

84

"It doesn't matter to me, Lorenzo. I won't be around to see it. Are you going to shoot me in the heart?"

I clear my throat and say, "In the head. It'll be quick and mostly painless."

Raina opens her eyes, and stares directly into mine, as I step closer to her and pull my gun from the back of my pants.

She opens her mouth to speak, but her trembling voice comes out soft and low.

"I'll be the ghost that follows you through your life. You'll never forgive yourself for this. You'll wonder if I hate you for killing me, but it won't matter, because you'll hate yourself far more than I ever could. I don't wish pain for you, but it'll be there. And just when you think you're moving past it, it'll ignite all over again, like a fire that just won't die. Nothing will extinguish it, because regret is a poison like cancer. It kills slowly, painfully. It eats away at you until there's nothing left. I'll be that for you."

Her words hit me in my chest. My breaths come out heavy, like I'm running, even though I'm standing perfectly still. I know her words are the truth. I'll never move past this moment. It's going to be a never-ending loop in my brain.

*Her vibrant green eyes staring into mine, like she can see straight to my soul.*

*The sound of her voice, begging me to not punish her for crimes she didn't commit.*

*Memories of the brat I wanted to tame, but had to kill, will never let me go.*

*She'll be the song I can't get out of my head.*

*The book I can't put down.*

*Some words stay ingrained in your brain. As much as you want to forget them, you never will.* We pay a price for being one of the most powerful families in the world.

And this is mine.

A solitary tear rolls down her cheek as she breathes.

"I'm ready, Lorenzo. Do what you need to do."

Gripping my gun in my hands, I point it to her head, holding it against her skin. She shivers, either from the fear, or the cool metal against her flesh, I'm not sure which. I stare into her eyes as much as I can, with the firearm obstructing my view. The last thing I want to do is look at the most beautiful woman I've ever seen, as I take her life away, but this is what she asked for. I can at least give her this.

"I'm sorry, beautiful Firecracker."

Life is funny. And tragic. It gives and it takes away.

Taking a deep breath, the self loathing fills me as I place my finger on the trigger. The smooth metal feels like a sharp knife cutting into my flesh. I pull the trigger. And so begins my destruction.

# Chapter Sixteen
## RAINA

I'm not sure who is more stunned that I'm still alive. Lorenzo stands staring at me, with an expression I'm not sure he's ever worn before. Shock. Disbelief. Shell-shocked.

"Fucking misfire," he says, I think, to himself.

"A fucking misfire," he repeats.

The Kage I know, although not well, is a man well controlled. He doesn't appear to lose grip easily, but right now he looks more like a man going insane, as I tremble, waiting for him to aim the gun and try again.

His chest expands with heavy and hard breaths, as he throws the gun against the wall in the bathroom. It goes off, a bullet hitting the wall, and he storms over to me. Both his fists and jaw are clenched, as he grits out his words.

"I cannot fucking go through that a second time."

Climbing on the bed, he straddles my hips and stares at me. His gaze is heated and captivating. I couldn't look away if I tried. I'm caught in the web of a venomous spider. Dangerous, lethal, but the way he looks at me, tells me he isn't going to make a second attempt.

He wraps his hand around my throat and, leaning his head forward, he growls.

"Fucking Abruzzos. Why the fuck did you have to be one of them? This could be so simple and instead, it's complicated. You're going to cost me everything."

"I'm sorry," I whisper, and it's not a lie. We're both caught in a situation I don't believe either of us wants to be in.

He takes my bottom lip between his teeth, and pulls on it before releasing his hold.

"You will be, Firecracker. You're mine now. I own you. This pussy. Your mouth. That sweet little asshole. All of you. Mine. Even your fucking soul."

My heart is pounding. It started when we got in here and has continued, but now it's out of control.

Reaching into his pocket, he pulls out a knife, and I freeze.

"Breathe, Firecracker."

He cuts down the center of the shirt I'm wearing, before he tosses the knife on the end table. Taking the shredded material, he opens it, baring my breasts to him, as he stares like he's never seen them before.

Leaning forward, he swipes his tongue across my nipple, causing me to shiver. He pinches the other one, as he speaks in a low, gravelly voice that speaks to my core.

"I think we need to get you some jewelry."

I glance at him, not knowing what he's talking about, and he chuckles softly.

"Nipple clamps."

I open my mouth to argue, but close it quickly, because I don't think I have a choice, and he already spared my life. What more can I ask for?

"Spread your legs."

I do as I'm told, and he slides down my body, quickly pulls his pants down, and lines his cock up with my entrance.

"I'm going to need to fuck you frequently, and you're going to let me, right?"

I roll my eyes and say, "Like I have a choice."

He pushes inside me with a sexy groan.

"You don't."

I don't know what he's doing when he sits up onto his knees.

"Legs on my shoulders."

Kage wraps an arm around my thighs and smirks at me.

"Hold on, Raina. It's going to be a wild ride."

I still don't know what he's talking about, but I figure it out when he starts fucking me hard, almost like it's a punishment. His fingers dig into the side of my thigh, as he watches my breasts bounce with every movement.

"Stunning. Fucking stunning. Play with your pretty clit."

My cheeks heat as I admit, "I've never done that."

He shakes his head as he pulls out of me, grabs my thighs and flips me to my stomach.

"Get on your hands and knees."

The second I'm in position, he slams back into me. Reaching underneath my stomach, he places his hand between my legs and rubs my clit.

"You will learn how to make yourself come, because I want to watch you get yourself off."

He begins to move inside me, and I can't stop the whimpers that slip out.

"Lorenzo."

"Fucking hell. Look how wet you are for this cock."

He pulls out most of the way, and pushes back inside me, hitting that spot inside me that makes me crazy.

I grip the plastic on the bed and dig my nails into it, as my pussy clenches down on his length.

"Good girl. Come all over my cock."

His words push me over the edge, as I cry out for him repeatedly. I glance over my shoulder as his breathing gets heavier, and watch his face as he loses himself inside me. He may be a monster, but he's beautiful when he comes. The way his jaw clenches, as the pleasure radiates on his face.

There's a knock at the door and we both freeze.

"Boss, I need to talk to you. It's urgent."

He pulls out of me, groaning in irritation.

"I'm going to fucking kill him."

Kage walks into the bathroom and comes out with a bathrobe.

"Put this on. Any man who sees you naked is a dead man."

I get off the bed and put the oversized fluffy white robe on, and he pulls his pants up before opening the door.

The man at the door opens his mouth to speak, but Kage holds his hand up.

"In a minute. Let me get her to the other room."

The man says, "But Boss."

"Just fucking wait," Kage says as he takes my hand, and we walk down the hall to his bedroom.

"I have to take care of whatever this is. I'm not going to put you in the cage. We'll call this a trust exercise. If you try to run, Raina, I will find you. Please don't make me hurt you."

I shiver at his tone, and wrap my arms around my waist as if trying to hold myself together. A habit I picked up as a child.

"I won't go anywhere."

"Good. Help yourself to anything in the room, but stay put."

He storms out the door, obviously angry we got interrupted. I feel kind of bad for the guy.

Grabbing the remote control, I turn on the television, and watch some stupid sitcom that looks like it's probably older than I am. I wait and wait for him to come back, but eventually fall asleep on his bed.

# Chapter Seventeen
## KAGE

I get out of my bedroom, and Pedro is standing there waiting for me, which only pisses me off more.

"Where's the fucking fire?"

He points down the hall.

"She's dead, sir."

"What? Who's dead?"

He raises his eyebrows and says, "The mother, Boss."

I quickly walk down the hallway, with Pedro moving beside me. "How?"

Maybe she had a heart attack. She wasn't being mistreated, and none of my men would've hurt her unless instructed to do so, and I sure as fuck didn't order it.

"She was shot. I don't know what happened, but a bullet came through the bathroom on the other side."

Jesus fucking Christ. When I threw the goddamn piece of shit gun, it fired.

"Are you sure she's dead?" I ask before entering the room.

"One clean shot right to the head. She's gone."

I stare down at her mother's dead body, and run a hand through my hair. This is something Raina will never get over. If she didn't already hate me, she will now. Forcing her to kill her father, no big deal, because she knew what a piece of shit he was. But her mother? It will take a goddamn miracle for her to get past this.

"Refrigerate the body."

The least I can do is let her decide what she wants done with her mother's corpse.

Jesus fucking Christ. How did my life get so out of control? I'm the guy that does what he wants when he wants, and answers to no one. The same man that doesn't give a shit about anybody's feelings. Yet here I am.

Fuck. I'm going to have to tell her I killed her mother, but not yet. She just saw her, so I'm hoping she doesn't ask to see her again for at least a few days. I'm not ready for the shitstorm this is sure to bring, especially because I haven't figured out how to handle my brothers quite yet. My life has gone from very controlled to complete chaos in an instant.

Funny thing is, I'm far more worried about her stabbing me than Psycho, but also kind of hope for it. I deserve it, even though killing her mother wasn't intentional. My phone buzzes in my pocket and I pull it out, glancing at the message I received.

**Bones:** *Checking in to make sure you aren't getting attached.*

**Me:** *Not attached.*

**Bones:** *Is she dead yet?*

**Me:** *No.*

**Bones:** *Get it done, Kage. For Reaper, if not for the rest of our family.*

**Me:** *Yes, Master.*

It's almost guaranteed, within the next forty-eight hours, I'll be summoned to his office for a conversation about this. I will have no choice but to give him an honest response, as to why she's alive, and whether or not I plan to kill her. I don't. I tried. Her mother's dead. Surely that has to count for something. I'll gladly kill every Abruzzo left walking the earth but her. Not her.

Another chime on my phone has me rolling my eyes.

92

**Bones:** *I want you at my house tomorrow night. If she's still alive by then, bring her with you.*

**Me:** *I said I'd handle it.*

**Bones:** *Not a request, brother.*

**Me:** *Alright. I'll see you and Athena tomorrow.*

**Bones:** *Just me. She won't be here.*

Fuck. There's only one reason she wouldn't be there. He's going to kill her, if I don't before then. Not showing up is not an option, because he'll just show up at my house. There is no avoiding this unless I run with her, and I'm not fucking running.

I take a deep breath, and head back to the woman I'm risking everything for. I'm not in love with her, so I have no idea if this is going to be worth it, but for some reason, I just can't take her life. It almost killed me when I had the gun to her head. I'm not a religious man, but if I were, I'd say a higher power stopped her from dying on that bed.

I walk back to my bedroom and find her curled up, in a deep sleep. She's breathtaking. Her bright red hair surrounds her, her lashes flutter slightly as she sleeps, and her lips are slightly parted as she breathes. The robe she's wearing has shifted in her sleep, and shows off her pale thighs. Fucking gorgeous.

Moving to the bed, I sit down gently as I continue to watch her. I could stare at her for days and never get bored. My reign as a decent human being ended with sparing her life, which, if I'm honest, may have been a selfish choice.

Standing up, I move her to her back, careful to not wake her. Undoing the tie on her robe, I open it and instantly harden. Fuck.

I stare at her and don't know where I want to taste first. Every inch is fucking perfection. My eyes stay on her as I remove my pants. After spreading her legs, I stare at her beautiful pussy. Bare and waiting for me. Climbing onto the bed, I slide inside her slowly, still trying not to wake her. She moans lightly, but doesn't wake up as I rock back and forth. Raina is instantly wet for me and feels like heaven.

Positioning myself over her, I place a hand on the mattress on either side of her head, and watch her pretty little mouth open slightly as she moans.

"No, Leo. Please, no," she whimpers.

Her eyes pop open as tears slide down her cheeks. She appears frozen, and I know from her words that she thinks I'm her disgusting uncle, so I stop, unsure of what to do.

Placing my hand on the side of her face, she finally blinks like she's transported back to the here and now.

"Firecracker," I say, my voice coming out as pained as my chest feels, as it threatens to squeeze the life out of me.

She lifts her hand up, I think to push me off of her, or at least try, but instead she places it on the back of my head, and pulls me closer for a kiss.

Her lips are soft, inviting, and perfect, but no more than her whimper that escapes into my mouth, as I slide my tongue against hers. Raina lifts her hips, as she grabs onto my hair with her small fingers, and pulls at the strands.

Pulling my hips back, I push forward, hitting her clit with my pelvis, and she moves her fingers to the base of my neck, digging her nails into my flesh, as she opens her mouth to cry out.

"Lorenzo," she nearly screams.

I don't know what I'm going to do about my brothers, but I'm not going to let them kill her. There's no chance of it. This beautiful woman is mine. We all have choices to make, and this is mine. If Bones makes the decision to push me out of the family, that's his.

I'll respect it, as much as it might destroy me. Whatever this is with Raina may not be what Bones has with Athena, but it's something, and I'm not letting this go.

Her back arches off the bed as she continues to cry out my name. It sounds like a chant, a prayer, and my name has never sounded so beautiful as it does falling from her lips.

# Chapter Eighteen

## RAINA

He flips over so I'm laying on top of him, and holds me against his chest.

"Tell me about *Leo*."

The way he says his name is with obvious hatred.

"What do you want to know?"

Kage drags his fingers through my hair as he kisses the top of my head.

"What he did to you."

"Lorenzo," I warn, because I don't want to talk about him.

"Tell me, Firecracker. He touched you, but never had sex with you?"

I cringe as the pain fills me once again.

"I had to stay a virgin, so my father could sell me like cattle. Leo knew that. He took everything other than my virginity."

He clenches his fists around my back, and his voice comes out low and threatening.

"I will make him pay. Trust me, he will regret every time he put his hands on you."

The tears are instant, and the emotion gets trapped in my throat as I squeak out, "You would do that for me?"

He flips me over to my back, and stares at me with a heat that I swear could burn me.

"You're mine. Any man who touches you, past or present, dies," Lorenzo adds through a clenched jaw, "Painfully."

I swallow hard as a tear slips down my face.

"Why are you crying?"

The truth twists like a knife in my stomach.

"Nobody has ever stood up for me. They never cared. Not even my mom."

"But you're close to her?" He asks with obvious confusion.

I squeeze my eyes shut tight, as the hurt nearly consumes me.

"I love my mom. It's the closest relationship I ever had, but it's complicated. My mother is the perfect mafia wife, and does as she's told, and turns a blind eye to the most revolting things. When my father and brothers had Bella in the basement, I said something, and her reaction was of dismissiveness, like I shouldn't even be surprised they were gang-raping a girl in the basement. Her husband was raping a girl, because of what her boyfriend did. And because she's a good mafia wife, she said nothing. We never could've prevented it, but she could've at least expressed her disgust, although I'm not sure she had any."

"It sounds like you don't like her much."

I open my eyes and smile at him.

"That part of her, I don't like. The other parts, I do. My father always favored my brothers. There was nothing I'd contribute to his empire, so it was always about them. My mom and I are close. She has always loved and supported me, when the rest of my family didn't care if I was even alive. She's my world. Thank you for not killing her."

# Chapter Nineteen
## KAGE

Fuck.

She's definitely going to stab me, and probably try to run away. Of course, I'll chase her to the ends of the goddamn earth, but I'd rather her stay willingly, like this. I should tell her and get it over with. Rip the *band-aid* off, so to speak, but I think I'd prefer to deal with that fallout after my brother's bullshit. One raging fire at a time, please.

"We have to go see my brother tomorrow. I probably need to get you some clothes."

She bats her eyelashes like she's trying to butter me up.

"My friend could bring me some. Please, Lorenzo. I promise I'll be obedient like you want me to be. I just want to see Casey."

I chuckle while I reach up and pinch her nipple.

"You know how to behave?"

Raina yelps before giggling softly.

"Only when I'm getting what I want."

The green in her eyes lightens as she smiles, and it makes my black heart come to life slightly. She does something to me that fucks with my head. It's uncomfortable, but I know I'll do just about anything to see her smile again.

"Your friend can bring you clothes, and you can spend time with her, but I'm trusting you, Firecracker. Don't do something to break it, because you may never get it back again. I won't be here, but my security team will be."

She throws her arms around my neck.

"Thank you, Lorenzo, thank you. I'll be on my best behavior, I promise."

I arch an eyebrow and say, "That'll sure be entertaining to see."

When she laughs again, I know I'm in trouble. I'm addicted to everything Raina. Her laugh, her smile, and her sweet pussy. Raina Abruzzo is a one person wrecking crew. I wanted to ruin her. Destroy her, and then end her life, but the tables have turned. I'm going to lose my family, when I tell my brother she's to stay alive. And when I tell her I killed her mother, somehow I'll lose her. I may physically keep her with me, but the way she is looking at me right now will come to an end.

Her stomach rumbles, and I arch an eyebrow.

"Time for you to get some food."

I get out of bed and throw some sweatpants on.

Pulling her off the bed, I do up her robe, because I wasn't kidding when I said any man that sees her naked dies. And it'd be a shame to lose any of my men.

"I'll heat up some lasagna for you."

She takes my offered hand and looks at me with surprise.

"You can cook?"

I chuckle as I shake my head.

"I said heat up. I did not say cook. My chef made it."

We walk into the kitchen, and I motion for her to take a seat at the island.

"Do I need to be worried about Bones?"

Here comes lie number one.

"No, of course not."

"Why is his name Bones?" She asks as I turn the oven on.

I sigh audibly, a little nervous about scaring her more than I'm sure she already is.

"We all deal with enemies differently. Bones breaks bones, Reaper kills people, for something to do, and Psycho enjoys using a knife. Blood is a thrill for him."

"And you?" She asks, as I set a wine glass in front of her.

I pour myself a glass as I consider whether or not I should tell her the truth.

100

"You don't want to know, Raina. Don't ask questions, if you aren't prepared to deal with the answers."

She lifts her gaze to mine, and her expression is serious.

"I want to know. I've probably seen worse. I'm prepared for the truth."

I walk away and put the lasagna in the oven. Taking a big gulp of my drink, I set it on the table and begin to tell my story.

"When we were kids, we got drafted into the family business at an early age. Too early, probably. I quickly found that I enjoyed watching someone in a cage. A person in a cage generally goes through stages. The first is freaking out. They search for any way to get free. Their eyes get wide as the panic sets in. You can almost see their hearts beating so fast they could have a heart attack."

She listens attentively, so I continue against my better judgement.

"Over time, it changes from crying, until they eventually act resigned. They know they'll die there. The hope vanishes. I enjoy seeing that process. The evolution of hope to hopelessness."

"That's how they die?"

I nod slowly.

"It's not always how I do it, but when I have time, I do. I enjoy the suffering."

She tilts her head to the side with, not horror, but curiosity.

"Is that what you were going to do to me?"

I shrug my shoulders and tell her the truth.

"I didn't know. I knew I wanted you in my cage, but I hadn't thought through how it would end."

Raina places her hands on her lap and speaks quietly.

"If you have to kill me, please don't do it like that. It takes weeks to starve to death, which is how I assume they die. Or days to die from dehydration. I'd prefer a bullet from a functioning gun."

I move closer to her, and take her face in my hands.

"I have no intention of killing you. Will you end up with the shock collar on again? Maybe. Will I spank you? Also a possibility.

I'm not interested in losing you. I don't know what the fuck this is, but I like having you with me, in my bed, in my house, and I'm not prepared to let you go."

She smiles at me, with a sparkle in her eyes, but her next words cause my heart to pound.

"Can I see my mom again soon?"

I keep my expression stoic, the way my father trained all of us, and here comes lie number two.

"Maybe. You're seeing your friend tomorrow. I'm not a kind man, Firecracker. Don't try to take advantage of my affection for your pussy. This is not a love affair. I kept you alive because I don't fuck corpses. I will tell you when you can see her again. Until then, I don't want to hear another word about it. Also, she's been moved further away from our end of the house, so tomorrow, when I'm trusting you here alone, don't look for her."

She quickly turns her head and avoids my gaze.

"I understand."

# Chapter Twenty

## RAINA

Just when I think there could be a heart under that rough exterior, he proves me wrong.

Any affection he has for me is because of what's between my legs. The same thing I've been told for most of my life. These mafia men see no worth unless it's something to fuck. The only reason I'm not telling him how much I hate him is because I want to see Casey tomorrow.

"Cat got your tongue, Firecracker?" He says as he places a plate of food in front of me.

I shake my head no, and pick up the fork and start eating, because I'm starving. And I don't really have a lot to say to him right now.

Kage folds his arms over his chest and stares at me with a heated expression, obviously not believing me.

"Raina, there is something on your mind. I can see the wheels turning."

I glance up at him and roll my eyes.

"You really have a way with women, Lorenzo. All women, everywhere, love knowing how much affection a man has for her pussy. I totally enjoy knowing I have no fucking use, other than for you to have somewhere to stick your dick. You may be from a different mafia family, but you're all the same."

Placing my fork on the plate, I look him in the eyes and say, "Spending the last twenty minutes with you has made me lose my appetite."

After getting up, with Kage staring at me, like he can't believe I had the guts to speak to him the way I did, I take care of my plate and head back to the bedroom. I listen for footsteps, with him following me and threatening to use the collar, or put me in the cage. But it never comes.

*The Next Morning…*

I stretch my arms as I wake, careful not to wake Kage as I stir. Opening my eyes, I notice he's not here. After climbing out of bed, I throw the bathrobe on and notice the time. Ten in the morning, and that means Casey will be here soon, or maybe he's already here. I need to hurry. Making my way into the bathroom, there's a note taped to the mirror that catches my eye.

*Firecracker,*

*I know you're mad at me, but don't forget you gave me your word. I do not trust easily and once it's broken, it's almost always permanent. If you betray me, you'll find yourself in the cage while wearing nothing but your necklace.*

*Behave,*
*Kage*

I yank it off the mirror, crumple it up, and toss it in the sink for him to find. Necklace. It's a fucking shock collar, not a piece of jewelry. I'm infuriated, but I try to ignore it, as I fix my hair to go see my friend.

My hand is on the doorknob, and when I yank it open, I come face to face with a man I don't know. He's big. No, he's massive.

Think the Incredible Hulk without green skin. He stares at me like I did something to offend him.

"Mr. Bonetti had business to conduct. Your friend is waiting downstairs for you. I'll escort you."

I glance at him with a raised brow.

"I know where it is. Thank you."

His hand grips my shoulder.

"I'll escort you. I've been instructed to keep my eyes on you at all times today."

I roll my eyes and say, "Whatever."

So much for trust.

As the hulk said, he escorts me, and watches every move I make. When I walk toward Casey with a smile on my face. When I hug him. When my robe slips open slightly. I have no doubt that Kage will receive a full report of everything I say or do. Best behavior indeed.

"Chica," Casey drawls in his southern accent.

He glances around at the hulk, and the man standing near the front door.

"Are you safe?"

I nod, because if I say no, there's nothing Casey can do about it. If he could've saved me from this life, he would've done it years ago.

"My father's dead."

He raises a brow and follows me to the kitchen, where I pour us both a cup of coffee. After adding the vanilla cream to both of ours, we start drinking it as we speak quietly.

I glance from hulk back to Casey.

"My brothers too."

"Hallefreakinglujah!"

I giggle until he says, "If this guy you're living with is responsible for that, I must meet him. He's my fucking hero."

I snort laugh. "He is not a hero."

"Anti-hero?" He questions.

Sipping on my coffee, I think before answering him.

"Straight up villain."

I'm quick to change the subject after that, because I don't want him to worry about me, and if I'm not careful, he will.

Casey places his arm around me, with an evil grin on his face.

"Ready for some drama?"

I nod excitedly.

"Hell yes, as long as it's not about me, I'm in."

Casey doesn't waste time filling me in on what's been going on with our small group of friends.

"Jason proposed to Abby, and she said yes, blah, blah, blah. Guess how they celebrated?"

I shrug, because I have no idea.

"A swingers' party with a gang bang."

My mouth hangs open in shock, as I look less than lady-like, and then I crack up laughing. As always we are having so much fun together, and when I hear his voice I feel myself shrink in fear.

"Get. Your. Fucking. Hands. Off. Of. What's. Mine."

# Chapter Twenty-One
## KAGE

I walk in and see this asshole with his hands on Raina, as she laughs differently than I've ever fucking seen. I've never witnessed that full body laugh. She's comfortable with this guy, whoever the fuck he is, and I don't like it. When I was a kid, they used to joke that my name should be Rage, not Kage. Psycho called me by that name for three years, until I locked him in a cage for four days. I never liked the name, but right now it's fitting, because I'm seeing red like I never have before.

I glance at my two security guys before focusing my attention back to Raina.

"Get out," I order, and as usual they're quick to obey.

"Step away from her. She's mine."

He moves to the side of the kitchen island with his hands up.

"On your knees."

"Lorenzo, stop," Raina says as she trembles with fear for this guy, but I ignore her, because I can't stop seeing his fucking hands on her.

"I won't tell you again."

He lowers himself to his knees, and I grab Raina by her hair and spin her around. She whimpers as I push her over the island, holding her with one hand, and unzipping my pants with the other. I look at this guy, who I'm now assuming is Casey, even though I thought Casey was a girl.

"You make her laugh. I make her come. We are not the fucking same."

I yank the bathrobe up and slam inside her, while holding her down by the back of her neck. I barely hear her whimpers. The most prominent sound is my pulse pounding in my ears. Raina trembles underneath me. I know she isn't afraid for herself, but him, and it only heightens my rage. I pull my gun from my holster on my hip and point it at his head, while I stay inside her.

"Nobody sees her like this. Only me."

Pulling the trigger, I hit him once in the forehead, and she screams as his body slumps forward on my expensive tile, and blood sprays from his wound.

"Get the fuck away from me," she cries, but I don't. Instead, I keep fucking her.

"Did I tell you what would happen to any man that touches you?" I grunt out.

"Fuck you. You killed my best friend."

I pull my hips back and slam forward repeatedly.

"That's right, and I'll kill a hundred more. Nobody touches you. And a new rule, nobody makes you laugh like that."

I pull out of her and grab her shoulders, and turn her to me. Her sobs are loud, as she occasionally looks over at her friend.

"You're a monster," she says between hiccups.

And she's not wrong.

Reaching down, I tuck myself back into my pants.

"I suggest you listen in the future, Firecracker. When it comes to other men touching you, I have no control. You know that now. Go upstairs and get ready. We're going to my brother's house."

She looks at me point blank, as she controls her sniffles.

"Mark my words, Kage Bonetti, I'm going to ruin you. Your destruction is mine. Somehow, someway, I will be your undoing. It's not a threat. It's a promise."

Raina storms off out of the kitchen and suddenly stops.

"He made me laugh like that because he was kind to me. Casey never treated me like I was property, whose only value was her pussy. Every time we were together, he made me happy. Something you could never do!"

And then she's gone, leaving me alone with my thoughts, ones I'd like to carve out of my brain with a knife.

This day keeps on getting better. After we get back from talking to my brother, I need to tell her about her mother, and I already know it's not going to go well. It wasn't intentional. Maybe that'll make her feel better about it.

*Fucking idiot. Nothing is going to make this news easier to hear.*

She stomps her feet as she moves toward me like a petulant child.

"What are you wearing? I thought your friend brought you clothes."

Raina raises an eyebrow.

"Oh, my dead friend? He did. I'm not dressing up for you. If you want a *Barbie,* I suggest you buy one."

I stare at her clothing and attempt to hide my laughter. She looks ridiculous, to say the least. Like an unkempt mess but still gorgeous. She's wearing a white t-shirt with splatters of paint all over it, like she wore it for redecorating, and for some reason never got rid of it. And the jeans she's wearing aren't much better. They look very worn. I'm not even sure a thrift store would take them. Did she bother to brush her hair? Definitely not.

I shrug my shoulders.

"If this is how you want to see my brother, then so be it."

"I'm not looking to impress the Bonetti scum."

"Nice," I say, as I grab her hand and pull her to the door.

She's quiet on the entire ride, and given the circumstances, I'm not surprised. Raina has an attitude that matches her hair to a 'T'. Her temper is even worse, but I'm not an idiot. I understand why she's upset. Hopefully, after I tell her about her mother, we can get the explosions out of the way and move on. Do I know that's really fucking unlikely? Yes, but a man can hope.

We pull into the gates in front of Bones' house, and security immediately lets me through with a nod.

I park and get out, walking around to her side, and can't help noticing the nearly black clouds threatening to pour down. A dark, ominous feeling surrounds me, like the gates of hell are closing in on me. Opening Raina's door, I help her out of my SUV, and she glares at me.

"I hate you," she whispers.

She has never spoken words more true than these to me. Her hate is visceral.

Pulling her into my arms, I hold her against my chest, and press my lips to the side of her face.

"I know you do."

She presses her face to my chest and cries. Her body shakes against mine, and I wrap my arms around her.

"Why?"

I place my finger and thumb on her chin and lift her head, forcing her gaze to mine, and sigh audibly.

"I can't handle a man touching you. It's something I'll never tolerate, Raina."

While I want to make her understand, I'm not sure I can.

"The rage was blinding. All I could see were his hands on you. And I reacted to it. I'd like to say it will never happen again, but it probably will, because you're fucking gorgeous, and men will want you, and not be able to control themselves."

I kiss her lips softly.

"Let's get this over with."

Releasing my hold on her, I take her hand and walk her into Bones' house, where Reaper is waiting. Are all my brothers here? This is unexpected, and has my hackles raised. After all, he did try to kill Raina once already.

# Chapter Twenty-Two
## RAINA

Reaper, the man who tried to kill me in the hospital, stares at me as we walk in. He's silent, but stares at me with an unreadable expression. His gaze moves from me to Kage, and I can instantly breathe again.

"Bones and Psycho are upstairs. They'll be down in a few minutes."

He waves to the expansive living room and says, "Have a seat."

Kage walks me over to the massive 'L' shaped black sectional, and we sit down. Reaper sits on the other side, with a leg crossed, and a dark expression on his face.

"How's Bella?" I ask.

Kage warns me in a low tone.

"Raina."

His brother glances at me before looking away.

"She's doing better. Her heart is still broken over our losing our baby boy. I don't know what the fuck is going on between the two of you, but I won't soon forget that your family killed my son. And what they did to my Living Dead Girl."

I don't really get the reference, but it's everything else he said that matters.

"I'm really sorry for what happened to her, and your baby. If I could've taken her place and saved him, I would have. I'm not proud to come from the family I come from. I take no joy in what happened to you, and for what it's worth, I'm glad they're dead."

He arches an eyebrow in surprise, and then says a simple, "Thanks."

Two voices echo somewhere upstairs, followed by feet moving down the steps. Kage speaks low.

"Maybe try to curb the attitude slightly."

I shift uncomfortably, because I don't know much about Bones, but he's the head of the family, and I assume he's going to have the final call about my life. I knew when Kage told me coming here was nothing to worry about it was a lie. We are not here for his brothers to get to know me. I might be more worried about Psycho. The name itself sends off warning signs, but I've heard stories about him from my brothers for years. A man that cuts his victims, and sews them up so he can continue his torture, is frightening. I've even heard that he's given people blood transfusions, so that he can keep up the torment for weeks at a time. Rumor has it that every Bonetti man is dangerous, but the thought of being butchered repeatedly sends chills down my spine. They both approach and take a seat. They look as lethal as I know they are, but there's something powerful in the Bonetti DNA. Each of them look like a woman's darkest fantasies coming true, other than the 'I might kill you' thing.

Bones rubs his thumb over his jaw, like he's deep in thought, before he speaks.

"I don't get it. She's an Abruzzo. Why the fuck is she alive?"

I can't help but shiver at his tone, dripping with hatred.

"Because she's mine," Kage says matter-of-factly.

Psycho sits on a chair opposite to the couch, spinning a knife in his hand. I wonder if it's to intimidate me. Someone should tell him I already am, and no further theatrics are required.

"There are close to four billion women in the world, and you pick an Abruzzo?"

Kage doesn't respond, and I don't think there's much of a response for that anyway, so his brother Bones continues, but turns his gaze to me.

"Is he holding you against your will?"

I tap my foot on the floor nervously, while I think of my response, and snap.

112

"You were there when he yanked me from my home. I think you know the answer to that."

He stares at me with a stoic expression, one that I think all the Bonetti brothers have perfected over time.

"Let me rephrase it for you, *Abruzzo.*"

The way he says my name, it's drenched with venom, like everything he needs to know about me is explained in that one word. As if he truly believes a person is defined by the family they were born into. There is little about me that matches my family. The comparison ends with physical features, but I don't bother trying to explain that to these men, because they wouldn't believe me anyway.

"If I told you that you were free to go, and let you walk out of here alone, would you?"

Kage grabs my hand, and tightens his around mine, like he thinks I might get up and run.

I shake my head no, and he visibly relaxes.

Bones smirks at me.

"I don't get it. Why?"

I'm sitting here with four mafia men, three of which want me dead, staring daggers into me, and I've never been great at controlling my tongue. Why start now?

"I don't know. Clearly I have a severe case of Stockholm Syndrome. I would bet money the Bonetti women have it as well, so perhaps you're familiar."

Bones glares at me, while Reaper and Kage sit still, like they're waiting for their brother to blow my head off, but Psycho laughs, like I told a hysterical joke.

"I like her," he says.

"Stand up, Raina," Bones says, with no emotion whatsoever.

Kage tightens his hold on my hand.

"Don't."

I glance at him.

"It's okay."

This is the second time I've been prepared to die. I'm okay with it, mostly.

Kage's voice is thick with emotion as I stand, emotion I didn't know he was even capable of.

"Bones, don't. Don't take away my light."

He shakes his head in disbelief.

"I still don't understand this. She's a fucking Abruzzo. And how can she be fine with you killing her mother?"

I turn to Kage, as the shock and terror bolts through me like a strike of lightning.

"You killed my mother?"

He admits it, "Yes, but it was an accident, Raina."

I back away from him, as my head screams to run as fast as I can, but his brothers all stand and surround me, like a lamb they're going to slaughter.

"You killed everything I love!"

The grief is overwhelming, a stabbing pain digs into my chest, as my heart squeezes with the knowledge I'll never see her again.

"Enough," Bones growls, "We had a plan. Every fucking Abruzzo. No exceptions."

He pulls his gun out and aims it at my head.

This is the end.

Once everything is taken from you, knowing you're about to die doesn't burn as much. The fear vanishes, because what do you have to live for?

Lorenzo Bonetti took everything from me. I look at him and say the last words I'll ever speak.

"I hate you."

Everything happens so fast, like someone pressed fast forward on my life.

Bones holds the firearm. His finger is on the trigger.

Reaper growls a loud no.

And he's in front of me as the gun goes off.

I'm knocked to the floor by the sheer force of him landing on top of me. The echoing howls of pain surround me, as the brothers realize Bones shot one of his own. He's pulled off me, and Kage presses his hand to my chest.

"Firecracker," he says, as anguish fills his expression, then his gaze moves to his brother.

"Reaper."

The darkness consumes me as I breathe my final breath, and my only thought is, I'm glad it's over. Death is freedom.

# Chapter Twenty-Three
## KAGE

Bones was quick to call our private ambulance service to get them both to our hospital. He currently looks as pale as a ghost. As much as I want to throw him through a wall, I say little, because I'm frantic about my brother and Raina's chances of survival. Bones went in the ambulance with Reaper. I am with Raina and Psycho in the other one. She's completely out, as the medic monitors her vitals, and keeps pressure on her chest.

"I still don't understand how they both got shot," I say, more to myself than anyone else.

Psycho says, "I think the bullet must've gone through Reaper, and into her. He only fired once."

"I can't believe this."

He arches a brow and shakes his head.

"And it's going to get worse after I fucking stab you."

As I watch Raina closely, I ask, "What'd I do to you?"

"We had a pact, asshole. You're in love with this girl, and you swore you wouldn't do the same shit the other two did. And look at you now."

I open my mouth to argue, but snap it shut because, fuck, I don't know. Maybe he's right. Am I even capable of loving someone? It doesn't really fucking matter anyway because if she lives, she hates me. And if she dies, I don't know how to get through it. If I'm lucky, when Psycho stabs me, and he will, he'll hit a vital organ.

"Sorry."

He chuckles softly.

"Yeah, I know you are. You're a sorry sack of shit. I hope she makes it, but I'm still going to stab you."

"Reaper better be okay."

Psycho grins.

"He'll be fine. You can't kill the Reaper. His little crazy already tried. Although she's probably going to kill Bones."

My brother might not be wrong. Bella is as crazy as Reaper is, and if we lose him, I'm not sure how she'll deal with it. Chances are more than good that she won't handle it well.

"Fuck, yeah. She's gonna be pissed even if he survives."

Suddenly a machine starts beeping, and two paramedics are on Raina.

"Her heart stopped," the one says, as the other starts CPR.

When they put paddles on her chest, and I watch her body jump from the shock, all the air leaves my lungs. Everything happens in slow motion, as the thread holding me together finally snaps. Every moment I've spent with her flashes through my mind. The pleasure and the pain. So much fucking pain I caused her. I swallow hard, as I watch the machine start to beep again. I breathe a sigh of relief, but know it could be short-lived. I could easily lose her still. I took everything from her. She might be laying on that stretcher thinking she has nothing to live for.

"Anything from Bones?"

Psycho shakes his head.

"Nope."

I have no idea if my brother is going to live, and if Bones killed him, I'm going to lose two brothers, because he will never be the same. Like me killing Raina's mother, it doesn't matter that it was an accident. Something like this you never get over.

Bones is my brother, but that won't save him from this. I will wait to make sure both of them will live, and then I'll deal with him. The only reason this happened is because he tried to take her from me. I don't give a fuck that he's the head of the family. Had he pushed me out, I would've walked away peacefully. Firing the shot that may very well kill Raina and Reaper? Fists are going to fly. If he weren't my brother, he'd be a dead man.

As if he can read my thoughts, Psycho says, "I'm not going to let you kill him, Kage. A few punches maybe, but the moment we make moves against each other, it's over. No matter what happens, we're family."

We arrive at the hospital, and the paramedics are quick to get Raina out of the back and rush her inside, while Psycho and I follow behind them. She is taken to a room and we stand, quietly observing, as I try to take in all their words, but fail miserably.

My brother nods slightly. "I'll be back with an update on Reaper, unless you need me to stay."

I shake my head no, because there's nothing he can do.

"Go," I say, and he does.

The doctor approaches me with a concerned expression.

"We're taking her to surgery. There's no exit wound, so the bullet is still inside her body."

"Can I talk to her first?"

He nods his approval, but warns me, "Only a minute. We don't have a lot of time."

She isn't conscious, so I don't know if she'll hear me, but I have to try.

I walk over to the bed, and stroke her arm, while staring at her angelic face. At this moment, I'd give anything to have her screaming at me again.

Kissing her softly on the lips, I stand back up and speak low, only for her to hear.

"Firecracker, I need you to make it through this. I know you'll never forgive me for what I did. Taking not only your best friend but your mom too. Fight through this and wake up, so you can give me hell. Please survive this, because I don't think I'll survive without you."

Leaning down, I whisper in her ear.

"I don't fucking know what love is, but whatever this is, I can't lose it."

119

A team of several medical professionals stand nearby, as the doctor clears his throat.

"We need to take her. Every minute we wait lessens her chance of survival."

I step away, and run a hand through my short hair, as they wheel her out of the room, leaving me with an emptiness in the pit of my stomach that grows by the second.

I walk out of the room to find out what the fuck is going on with Reaper. Psycho never came back, so I'm not sure what that means. It's not hard to find the room, with a mass of men outside guarding it. They recognize me, and move away from the door so I can enter.

As I make it into the room, I realize my brother, Reaper, is not here, which can only mean one thing.

"Surgery," Psycho says, answering my unasked question.

He sits on the chair beside where the bed normally goes, and Bones is sitting beside him, but Bella stands in front of Bones, with anger radiating all around her. I might not even get my shot with him. She holds her hand out to Psycho.

"Let me see your knife."

He chuckles loudly.

"Not today, Living Dead Girl. One brother on an operating table is enough for one day."

Bones stares at her with an arched eyebrow.

"It was a fucking accident. I never meant to shoot my own brother."

She folds her arms over her chest.

"I'm so tired of this family. Look at what you've cost me. I already lost our son, and now Nico? How will I go on without him?"

Bones rises from his chair and takes her into his arms, showing a softness normally reserved for his wife, Athena.

"I'm sorry. He'll pull through, because he has faced worse, and he has a lot to live for. If the day ever comes where he's not around, we'll take care of you, because you're one of us. You're part of this family, whether you like it or not. And we protect our own."

She cries in his arms as Athena walks through the door, and stares at Bella with Bones. She covers her mouth with her hand, obviously thinking the worst. Her and Reaper are very close. Probably as close as Bones would ever allow.

# Chapter Twenty-Four
## KAGE

Athena and Bella step to the side as they talk amongst themselves, and I glance at Psycho as he plays with his knife, spinning it in his hand, pressing his fingertips against the pointy part of the blade. I step up to Bones and glare at him.

"I told you she was mine. And you fucking shot her."

He rises quickly, and stares coldly into my eyes, without needing to move his head, since we are nearly the same height.

Bones clenches his fists at his sides, and I arch an eyebrow in question.

"Are you going to hit me?"

"No," he says flatly.

"What would you do if I shot Athena?"

He shrugs his shoulders as he narrows his gaze at me.

"It's not the same. She's my wife. And Raina is the enemy's daughter."

I lift my arm up and pull my fist back and pause, giving him a chance to take it back, but he doesn't.

Athena screams as I punch my brother in the face. I hit him again, and he continues to stand there, not trying to move or strike back.

His wife rushes over, but he holds his hand up, telling her to stop.

"Let him get it out."

This is how I know he is aware of how badly he fucked up. Bones is nobody's punching bag. I rub my fist as I stare at him.

"This is over, Bones. From now on, you'll stay away from Raina. I don't give a fuck that you don't like the family she's from. If you want ours to stay intact, with all of your brothers, then you'll never touch her again."

I can't bring myself to utter the words that are in my head. The ones that say if she dies, I walk away on my own, because I'll never be able to look at him again.

Three hours later, a female doctor walks into the room.

"Mr. Bonetti is in recovery. I expect him to make a full recovery."

She looks at me with a sad expression.

"Dr. Michaels is waiting in Ms. Abruzzo's room to speak with you about her condition."

Everyone celebrates the good news about my brother. Bella falls into an embrace with Athena. Bones glances at Psycho with a rare grin. Me, on the other hand; my heart is in my throat, as I make my way back to her room, feeling like what a man on death row must feel like, when he walks to the electric chair.

I walk in and find the dark-haired man standing with a stressed expression. If she's not alive, he should be terrified. Everyone should be, because I'll lose my mind. We may end up with two serial killers in the family.

"Ms. Abruzzo-"

"Raina," I interrupt, because much like my brothers, I hate that she has that fucking last name.

He nods his understanding.

"Raina suffered serious injuries. At this time she's in a stable condition, but that could change at a moment's notice."

The bile in my throat nearly chokes me, as I croak out my burning question.

"Will she live?"

He shakes his head slightly.

"We are doing everything we can but I cannot make any guarantees. The bullet penetrated her chest, before traveling to her pectoral muscle, creating a hole that allowed air to escape into the pleural space, causing her lung to collapse. She has a chest tube inserted into the chest cavity to drain the air, and allow her lung to re-expand. We will be watching her closely for signs of infection. I'll

124

have a better idea of her prognosis after these next forty-eight hours. She is on heavy sedation, so she'll be in and out of it for several days."

His words are not reassuring. Instead, they make me feel like this is goodbye, and I'm not ready for that. I'm not sure I ever would be. A collapsed lung sounds bad.

"Can I see her?"

He nods his head.

"Soon. She's in recovery. Raina will be brought here when she's out, and you can see her then. I know you have a big family, but two visitors at a time, and that's only because you're a Bonetti. It should be one."

"Thank you, Dr. Michaels."

Psycho walks in and stares down at the floor.

"I heard. I'm sorry."

We both look at the doorway as Bella walks in, and tilts her head to the side, when she sees the surprised expression on my face.

She looks much better after finding out Reaper will be okay. I wish I felt that same relief.

Bella glances around the room.

"She's not back yet? I wanted to talk to her."

Holding her hands up like she means no harm, she says, "Nothing bad. I swear."

"It might be a while before she can talk. She's on heavy sedation, and I don't even know if she's going to make it."

Once she reaches me, she hugs me tightly.

"I'm sorry, but she's going to make it. I know she will."

I chuckle softly as I step back from my brother's girl.

"How could you possibly know that?"

She smiles brightly.

"It's not optional. She's the light to your darkness. Like I am, to Nico."

Psycho laughs loudly.

125

"Maybe that's how it started, but now I'm not sure you're any less dark than my brother. After all, it wasn't so long ago that you asked for my knife to kill my brother."

She snorts as she rolls her eyes.

"I was not going to kill him. Just stab him."

Psycho looks at me, with his knife in his hand, and says, "I haven't forgotten. I'm still going to stab you. I'm just being considerate and waiting."

My attention snaps to the door, before I get a chance to thank him for his generosity, as they push Raina on her bed through the door. She looks pale as a ghost as she sleeps. This cannot be a good sign.

The nurse looks up at us with a scowl.

"There are too many people in this room. Dr. Michaels said no more than two at a time. One of you needs to leave."

Bella says, "I'll go. I'll check in later when she's awake."

Before she leaves, I ask, "Any idea why Reaper jumped in front of the bullet meant for her, like a goddamn superhero?"

She smiles. "He had his reasons, but I'll let him tell you what they were."

# Chapter Twenty-Five
## KAGE

"I'll leave you alone with your girl for a bit."

I nod, and Psycho walks to the door, before he stops and looks at me with a smirk.

"Any preferences?"

I shake my head in confusion.

"On what?"

"Body part when I stab you. I'm getting excited just thinking about it."

I groan in irritation.

"Preferably nothing vital. Fucking Psycho."

He grins like his name is an award, one he wears proudly.

"That's my name."

After he leaves, I go sit in the chair beside Raina's bed and watch her closely. The machine beeps, reassuring me that her heart is beating in a regular pattern. She has a breathing tube under her nose, as well as the tube in her chest, an IV in her arm, and if I'm honest with myself, she doesn't look alive. The machines are the only thing convincing me that she is. Seeing her like this causes my stomach to knot with guilt. Her words echo in my brain.

*"Every time we were together, he made me happy. Something you could never do!"*

I take her hand in mine, her skin too cool, and I talk to her, even though I have no fucking idea if she'll hear a word I say.

"Raina, I know I did some fucked up shit. Things normal men don't do, but I'm not normal. I'm not sure that I'm even capable of giving you the things you need. I know how to do three things. Fucking, killing, and causing tremendous suffering. If I were capable of more, I'd do the right thing and let you go. I know that's what you really want. Part of me wants to, so you can be happy, but, baby, I can't. I can't promise you much, but I'll try to be less of an asshole."

I kiss the back of her hand, and she stirs, but she doesn't wake up.

"I knew it." I hear from behind me, and the second I realize it's Bones, I jump up out of the chair ready for a fight.

He holds his hands up, trying to calm me.

"I came to talk. I'm not here to hurt anyone."

Against my better judgement, I point to the second chair beside her bed.

"Sit, but I'm warning you, Bones. I don't give a fuck who the head of this family is. If you hurt her, poor Athena will have to bury her husband."

He rubs his thumb across his jaw as he sits.

"And I'm warning you, Lorenzo, you will speak to me with respect. I'm going to forget what you just said to me, because I know you're upset and, hearing what you just said to Raina, I understand why."

I stare at him with confusion, because I don't know what he's talking about, and he chuckles softly.

"Well, shit. You don't even know why you're so upset, do you?"

Shrugging my shoulders, I don't respond, because what am I supposed to say?

"You're in love with her, Kage."

I keep watching Raina for some signs of life, while I talk to my brother, but so far there are none.

"I don't know what I am, Bones, but I'm not you. It's something I'm not sure I'm capable of, and I haven't even known her for that long."

He sits back in his chair, and crosses one leg over the other, as he continues rubbing his thumb along his jaw.

"I think I fell in love with Athena the night I found her, hanging upside down from my barbed wire. I didn't know it immediately, but the first time I saw her. Fuck. I was blown away."

128

Cocking my head, I stare at him while I think out loud.

"That's what it was the first time I saw her. We see beautiful women all the time. Perfect face, perfect body, but with Raina, it was different. Like some force outside myself I couldn't control pulled me to her. Like a goddamn powerful magnet. You know I almost killed her."

"What?" He says in a state of shock.

I shake my head at the painful memory.

"Yeah. I got the bed in one of the guest bedrooms prepared with plastic. She knew she was going to die. I promised to make it quick, and she laid there as I held the gun to her beautiful forehead, and pulled the trigger. Fucking misfire."

"Jesus, Kage. Why? You clearly love her. Why would you kill her?"

I shrug my shoulders.

"I had orders. I was following them."

"Fuck," he says, as he drags a hand down his face.

"I said all Abruzzos had to die. If I had known you weren't just fucking her, like you normally are with women, I would've handled it differently. What happened after?"

I sigh heavily.

"I threw the gun in a fit of anger and it discharged, killing her mother. And then I fucked her."

Bones arches an eyebrow.

"I didn't find out she was dead until afterward. That's when I told you."

We both sit quietly as she begins to stir again, and don't speak until she settles. The doctor did say she'd be in and out of it. Maybe this is what he meant.

"That's why she said you kill everything she loves? Or did she mean her father and brothers?"

I groan as I cover my face.

"No, she was talking about her best friend. I killed him earlier, and then you told her about her mom, so that was what she was referring to."

"Jesus, Kage. Women can get over a lot, but that's, I don't even know what the fuck you call it, more than a lot."

I nod in agreement.

"Maybe Athena and Bella can sweeten her up toward you. I know Athena helped Bella before."

Rolling my eyes, I chuckle.

"I don't know if I want Bella anywhere near Raina. She might turn her into a serial killer, and I'm positive I'd be her first kill."

She whimpers in her sleep, and Bones squeezes my shoulder.

"I'm going to go and let you have some time with her. It looks like she might wake up soon, and I don't need to be the first ugly face she sees."

Raina's eyes flutter slightly, but then they stop again, like she was waking up but fell back asleep.

Nurses come and go. The hours on the clock tick by and there's no change. I dig her phone out of my pocket when I feel it vibrate.

**Satan:** *Principessa, I miss you.*

I text Psycho the number, and ask him to find out who this fucker is. I have my suspicions, but I need confirmation to be certain.

# Chapter Twenty-Six

## RAINA

I open my eyes and see Kage sitting beside me, one of the last four people I'd want to see, as I wake up after being shot. He stares at me with an emotion filled expression, and I know it's fake, because Kage has none. The man that murdered both my best friend, and mother, cannot possibly feel a damn thing.

"Baby," he says, as he takes my hand and I pull it away.

I shut my eyes tight, so I don't have to look at him, and whisper, "Get me some water, please. My throat hurts."

He nods, and quickly runs out of the room like it's on fire, coming back with a nurse. She hands me a cup of water with a straw in it.

"Slow sips, Ms. Abruzzo."

I do as she says, but it's challenging, because I want to gulp it. I'm so fucking thirsty, it feels like I haven't had a drink in months, and makes me think about the people that have died in his cages. Is there more than one? If not, why his bedroom? Is it because watching people die gets him off? I stop drinking at that thought, because suddenly I feel sick.

The nurse checks my vitals and smiles at me.

"Dr. Michaels will be in to check on you soon."

She leaves, and I do everything I can to avoid his stare.

"Raina, please look at me."

"I can't, Kage. It makes me sick when I do."

Out of the corner of my eye, I see him put his face in his hands, revealing a Kage I've never seen, but at this point I'm detached. It's all been too much.

"I'm sorry about your mom. I didn't know when I threw the gun it'd discharge, and go through the fucking wall and hit her."

"And Casey?"

He groans like it's painful, but admits, "I meant to kill him."

Exactly as I thought. There's no remorse in his tone, but I didn't expect there would be.

"I'm tired. Can you go? I can't sleep with you here."

He rises from his chair and leans down, kissing me on the forehead, and says, "This isn't over, Raina. Somehow we're going to get through this, because I need you."

I look at him this time, but only to glare at him.

"I don't need you, Kage."

He turns and walks out of the room, and throws over his shoulder.

"I know you believe that right now, but it's a lie. I'm going to check on my brother, but I'll be back."

As Kage walks out and disappears, I'm left with the question of why in the world Reaper jumped in front of me. Why he tried to take the bullet meant for me. That doesn't make any sense. After all, he blames me, along with the rest of my family, for the death of his son, as well as the torture Bella went through.

Eventually thinking becomes too hard, and I close my eyes and fall asleep.

"Ms. Abruzzo," a quiet voice speaks, sounding far away.

I open my eyes to a beautiful brunette staring at me.

"Yes?" I ask, without having a clue who she is.

"My name is Anastasia Crowne, and I think we can both help each other out."

I roll my eyes at her.

"I don't think I'm in the condition to help anyone right now."

She hands me a card, and I hold it up with my hand that doesn't have an IV in it.

132

I arch an eyebrow at her.

"ADA? Assistant District Attorney?"

She nods slowly and glances behind her, probably to make sure we're still alone.

"I'm the new ADA, and I have every intention of taking the Bonettis down. I know you are not with Lorenzo Bonetti willingly. Help me. Give me what I need, and they'll go to prison for life, and you'll get your freedom."

Now she has my attention. When I told Kage I'd destroy him, this is not what I meant, but also it works. Part of me feels bad for Reaper, since he tried to save my life for some unknown reason, but right now I have to put myself first.

"What do you need?"

She smiles softly.

"Whatever you have."

I tell her the truth.

"I don't know how much help I'll be. They are a mafia family. I know they deal in drugs and trafficking."

She stares at me in interest, like she's hanging on my every word.

"Trafficking? Human trafficking?"

I can see that she thinks she hit the jackpot, but I shake my head.

"Weapons. I don't think they are in the trafficking of people, or even prostitution."

She glances behind herself again, before returning her gaze to me.

Reaching into her pocket, she pulls out a phone, and hands it to me.

"This is a burner phone. My number is speed dial one. I promise, I'll get you out of this, and you'll never have to worry about the Bonettis again."

After she leaves, I smile for what feels like the first time in a long time. A glimmer of hope. That's all I need to get through this.

I look around, trying to figure out where I can hide this phone. When I hear Kage talking to someone in the hallway, I quickly tuck it behind my back and close my eyes, so he thinks I'm still sleeping.

# Chapter Twenty-Seven
## KAGE

Her eyes open as I take a seat beside her, but she doesn't say anything.

"Raina, I'm sorry. I don't say that very often, but I'm saying it to you because I mean it. I'm so fucking sorry that I ended your mom's life. If I could take it back, I would. Hell, if I could take back ever pressing that fucking gun to your head, I would."

"And Casey?" She asks.

I shake my head.

"I'm sorry you're upset, but I'm not sorry that you won't be hanging around a man that you looked at like he was a goddamn hero. Something I could never compete with."

"He was my friend, and only my friend. My life was mostly miserable. I had two people that made it bearable, and, intentional or not, you took them both from me."

I try to change the subject, since we are going to keep going round and round, and getting nowhere. I'm not sure she'll ever forgive me. If she does, that time is certainly not now.

"How are you feeling?"

She rolls her eyes and says, "Like I got shot in the fucking chest."

"Do you need more pain medication?"

"How's your brother?" She asks, instead of answering my question.

"He's okay. Your injuries are worse."

Her eyes close, and I know that's the end of our conversation for now, so I sit and do the only thing that provides me comfort. I stare at her. Any solace I feel washing over me is short-lived, as thoughts of how I've hurt her circle around my brain. I'm a bad guy and I do bad things. I don't know any other way to be, but I don't like the way she sees me now. Even when I had the collar on her, threatening to shock her, she didn't look at me how she does now. When Raina opens her eyes again, I know the first thing she'll think, once again, is how I've taken everything from her. I'm not sure how to change that, but I do know I'm sure as hell going to try.

Rising from my chair, I lean down and kiss her on the forehead, and head back to my brother's room. I walk in and find both of my other brothers sitting in chairs on their phones, while Athena and Bella sit on the sides of Reaper's bed, talking to him.

"I need to talk to Athena."

Reaper narrows his gaze at me.

"Aren't you going to ask me why I did it?"

I chuckle as I step closer to the bed.

"I thought you were auditioning for the new Superman movie."

Pulling a chair closer to his bed, I take a seat, and look at him with a serious expression.

"Alright. Why?"

He pulls Bella against his side while he talks, and for the first time, watching them together has me feeling jealous, which is an unknown feeling for me. I've never been bothered watching either him or Bones with their women.

"You're in love with her."

I arch a brow as I sit back in the chair, trying to make sense of his words.

"So you took a bullet for her?"

My brother is a fucking serial killer. Lives ending is not a hardship for him, in fact, it's a thrill, so for him to put himself in harm's way for her still isn't adding up in my brain.

He shakes his head as he chuckles.

"I did not intend to take a bullet for her. My plan in that second, before the bullet was racing toward my chest, was to step in front of her."

He glares at the shooter. "And that it would stop Bones from killing her. Never in a million years did I anticipate he'd fucking shoot me. I saw the way you looked at her. It's the way Bones looks at Athena, and probably the way I look at Bella. If she had been the one to kill our son, I'd have let her die, but she didn't. She didn't hurt Bella, and she didn't hurt our son. Her only crime was being born. But I didn't do it for her, I did it for you."

I glance over at Bones and ask, "Care to explain why you shot our brother?"

He groans like he's annoyed by the question, since I'm sure he's been over this with the others already.

"I already had my finger on the trigger when Reaper moved in front of Raina. My brain didn't have the chance to realize Reaper was in front of the gun until I had already fired."

Sighing audibly, I say, "None of it even matters, because she hates me."

Psycho rises from his chair in annoyance.

"I'll be back. All this fucking love bullshit is making me crave blood. Besides, I think my victim misses me."

Athena giggles, as she walks back into the room carrying two trays of coffee. She hands Psycho his first, with an affectionate smile.

"I literally cannot wait for you to fall in love."

He takes the coffee, but looks at her like she's more insane than the rest of us.

"Never gonna fucking happen. I will stab *myself* if it does."

He looks over at me.

"Somewhere fucking vital."

Bones pipes up, with a questioning expression.

"Who's the victim?"

Psycho takes a sip of his coffee, as Athena passes each of us our own.

"Name is Diana, but apparently her friends call her Didi. Pretty girl, but she fucked up."

Bones nods knowingly, like he knows what he's talking about, as soon as he says the girl's name, but I don't, so I ask about it.

"What did she do?"

Psycho grins, like he can see her blood dripping from where he stands in this hospital room.

"Snooping around where she didn't fucking belong."

Bella appears to be practically salivating, and there's no doubt she's my brother's perfect match.

"Gonna kill her today?"

He shakes his head in response.

"Not a fucking chance. She's got weeks to go."

Psycho walks to the door and I stop him.

"Hey man, make sure all the torture doesn't make you forget what I asked you to do."

He nods. "I'm on it."

With a grin, he looks at me before he leaves.

"Stab ya later, brother."

Athena climbs onto my brother's lap, and he wraps his arms around her while he murmurs, "Butterfly," into her ear.

He looks over at me and nods.

"Talk."

She glances at me while she sits in his arms. "What's up, Kage?"

"Is there a way to make a woman not hate you? If you've done bad things?"

"How bad?" she asks, and Bones chuckles while filling her in on recent events. She stares at me in shock.

"That's bad, Kage."

I don't respond, because what can I possibly say? I know it's fucking bad.

Athena glances at Bella, then back to me with a soft smile on her face.

"All hope is not lost, Kage. I think I can speak for both Bella and I, when I say we've had our share of bad behavior to deal with. But!"

She holds up her finger and points at me.

"You need to curb that behavior now. Treat her like a person. Do things girls like, and maybe stop killing people she cares about."

Everyone laughs when I ask, "What do they like?"

Reaper says, "You're a lost cause."

Athena grins, like she knew I had no idea what women want, and she's not wrong.

"Flowers, date nights."

Bella interrupts her, "And orgasms. We really like those."

# Chapter Twenty-Eight
## RAINA

I wake up to Bella and Athena staring at me, and I'm immediately uncomfortable as fuck. I'm not sure what they want, but I assume the worst. Oh my God. Do they know about the ADA?

*Chill, Raina. Breathe. Don't make it so obvious.*

The brunette smiles softly, "I'm Athena."

Bella giggles at my confused expression, because I'm not sure why they're here.

"She's Bones' wife."

I arch an eyebrow. "Ah yes, my almost killer."

If my words bother her, she doesn't show it.

"How are you feeling?" Athena asks.

"Okay, I guess. I still have some pain, but it's getting better. The doctor took the chest tube out, and my lungs seem to be functioning again. Now, I'm just waiting to see if your husband is going to shoot me again. I may not be so lucky next time."

Her blue eyes focus on mine, like she's trying to be sure I'm listening to her words.

"Luca isn't going to hurt you."

"Luca?" I ask.

Bella answers for her.

"They all go by nicknames. Bones is Luca, Reaper is Nico, Kage is Lorenzo, and Psycho's real name is Massimo, but I suggest not calling them by their real names. Except Kage, for you, because it tends to be something only their women get away with."

Athena giggles as she adds, "Sometimes Luca will first name them if they are pissing him off."

I know, as I look at them both, that I don't fit in. We are not the same, not at all. Both of these women are pictures of happiness. Everything I'm not.

"I'm tired. I need to get some sleep."

That's a lie. I'm wide awake, but that's my go to now when everything begins to be too much, which seems to be almost always lately.

They both rise from their seats, and Athena places her palm over the back of my hand and squeezes gently.

"He loves you. I know the Bonetti men aren't great at showing it with actions, and I'm not sure he even realizes it yet, but he does."

I gaze at her as a tear rolls down my cheek.

"If that's love, I don't want it. His version of love has me feeling like I'm suffocating. It's cruel, and painful. Love doesn't torture. I think you're wrong. He hates me as much as I hate him."

She doesn't respond to what I said, she just looks at me with sad eyes.

"Get some rest, honey. We'll check on you later, if that's okay?"

I turn my head away from her gaze.

"I'd prefer you didn't. Really, I just want to be left alone."

She takes her hand away from me, clearly understanding.

"Of course, Raina. Take care of yourself."

They both seem nice, but they are Bonettis. I cannot risk developing a friendship, when I'm going to help the district attorney's office take them down. The women likely won't go to prison, but we won't be on friendly terms after I take everything from them. I'll be the person that costs them their entire world. That automatically makes me enemy number one. Friendship will only make it more difficult than it already is.

The nurse brings in a tray of food, and sets it on the table, before moving it in front of me. I look at the disgusting food that nearly makes me sick. Salisbury steak that looks like it's been reheated a thousand times. Mashed potatoes that I'd bet money are instant. Nothing looks appetizing beyond the cup of water.

"Thank you," I say as she walks away. I'll be polite, but I'm not eating this crap.

Two hours later, Kage walks in like he's ready to kill me, with his hands fisted and a scowl on his face.

"Why the fuck are you refusing to eat?"

I roll my eyes.

"I'm not."

He arches an eyebrow. "So the medical staff is lying to me, when they say you haven't eaten in two days?"

I shrug my shoulders, as I continue to flip through the magazine one of the nurses brought for me.

"Use your goddamn words, Raina. Why are you not eating?"

I glance up from the entertainment trash I'm not even really reading, and snap at him.

"Because the food tastes like fucking shit, that's why. If I get hungry enough, I'll eat it. Alright?"

He visibly relaxes as he sits in the chair beside my bed, and stares at me with a look I don't quite understand.

"Why didn't you tell me?"

I go back to turning the pages in the magazine.

"Why would I tell you anything, Kage?"

He doesn't say anything, he just keeps staring at me, like he can see right through my clothes. I lay the magazine on my lap, and cross my arms over my chest, while he smirks at me.

"Are you cold, Firecracker? Or are you just happy to see me?"

My glare is instant, as I say, "I'm definitely not happy to see you, Kage. That will never be the case."

He rises from his seat and places his hand on my throat, as he stares at me with a fire in his dark eyes.

"It's Lorenzo. My fucking name to you is Lorenzo. Now what do you want to eat?"

"Nothing," I whisper as I stare back at him, wishing my body wasn't heating up, at his close proximity.

"So I'm eating alone then, baby? Is that how it's going to be?"

I lay frozen, trapped in his intense gaze. "I guess so, because I don't want to eat right now."

He releases his light hold on my throat and walks over to the door, closes it, and locks it. Well, shit. I didn't realize it had a lock. Had I, I would've locked him out already.

"What are you doing?"

Grabbing the hem of the hospital gown I'm wearing, he yanks it up, revealing my naked body.

"Stop. What are you doing?"

Kage runs his tongue over his bottom lip.

"Eating my way to your heart, baby."

Pushing my legs open, he groans softly.

"Such a pretty pussy."

I warn him, "Kage, we are in a hospital. I'm sure somebody has a key. They could come in and see this."

He chuckles. "They could. What happens when someone sees what's mine, Firecracker?"

"They die," I whimper, as he leans down and slides his tongue up my slit.

Licking his lips, he grins, "Good girl. See, you're learning the way it is, baby. Now be my good girl and come all over my face."

# Chapter Twenty-Nine
## KAGE

"You can't even help yourself, can you?"

My gaze travels up her body, slowly taking in every inch of perfection.

"When it comes to you, not a chance."

"Oh fuck," she whispers, as I flick my tongue over her clit.

She's fucking gorgeous like this. While I devour her pussy, the hatred evaporates from her face, replaced with intense desire. Raina can pretend she feels nothing for me, but she's wrong. We at least have this, to break down her defenses.

Digging her fingers into the sheets on the bed, she whimpers as I push two fingers inside her, while I suck on her swollen clit.

"I hate you, Lorenzo," she cries out, as her back arches off the bed, causing me to chuckle lightly. She may hate me, but she does not hate what I'm doing to her.

Glancing up at her, I fuck her with my fingers, knowing I'm hitting her 'G' spot repeatedly.

"I know you hate me, Firecracker, but this ravenous pussy fucking loves what I do to it."

"No," she says in an angry tone.

"Yes, baby. Look how drenched you are for me. Do you hear the filthy sounds your beautiful cunt is making for me?"

Her cheeks go from pink to red, but she doesn't argue with me, because we both know what I said was the truth.

I get on the bed between her legs on my knees, and unzip my pants.

"What are you doing?"

Stroking my cock in my hand, I say, "Giving you what we both know you need."

She shakes her head. "I just had surgery, Kage."

I push inside her pussy, and groan at the feeling of her wrapped around my length.

"Then be a good girl, and lie there and take it. I'll be gentle."

Honoring my word, I pull my hips back and slide inside her at a slow pace.

She tightens around me, and her eyes nearly roll back into her head, as she comes undone for me. Only for me.

"Lorenzo. Fuck. Goddamn it."

I grip her thighs and dig my fingers into her beautiful flesh, as I drive into her, probably harder than I should be, but my control is limited with her.

"More, Firecracker. Give me more."

"Haven't you had enough?" She breathes heavily, and I slow my thrusts down.

Pulling out of her, I tuck myself back into my pants, and wedge myself beside her on the bed, laying on the edge as she bites, "I hope you fall."

Placing my hand on the side of her face, I turn her head toward me.

"I'll never get enough, Raina. Not in a million fucking years. You're under my skin, somehow you sewed yourself into the fabric of my soul, and now I can't see a damn thing other than you."

"Lorenzo," she breathes.

I shake my head.

"Let me finish. I need to just say this."

Her green eyes stare into mine, and I was worried about her heart when I should have been worried about my own. Mine beats out of control when she looks at me like this. Like for a moment, she doesn't wish for my death.

"I love you, Raina. I fucking love you, and I know I messed up, and I promise you, I will again."

I take a deep breath and exhale slowly.

146

"But I'll also make sure nobody ever hurts you again."

A tear rolls down her cheek, letting me know she's at least hearing my words, and not blocking them out.

"How can you possibly know that?"

"I know because I'll kill anyone that tries. Without hesitation, I'd lay down my fucking life to protect yours."

"Lorenzo, stop."

"Stop what?" I ask.

She lowers her head as more tears fall.

"Making it hard to hate you, when it should be the easiest thing in the world."

Those are the most beautiful words I've ever heard. I didn't expect her to say she loved me back. In fact, I knew she wouldn't. If she had, it would've been a lie. Saying she's having trouble hating me is the greatest gift right now.

I press my lips to hers and she's hesitant, but doesn't turn away from me. Pushing my tongue into her mouth causes her to whimper, as she reaches a hand up and tugs on my hair. I place my finger and thumb on her chin, and tilt her head back, exposing her pretty little throat to me, and place soft kisses on her skin.

"Fucking exquisite. And mine."

I scrape her flesh with my teeth, and she moans loudly.

The sounds she makes drive me to the brink of insanity, it's breathy and needy. I brush my fingers over her nipple, and groan when she makes more noise for me.

Her stomach growls louder than her moans, and I pull back from her.

"Tell me what you'll eat."

She tilts her head, and I can see the snarky comment before she even opens her mouth. Fucking brat.

"Lobster. I want lobster."

I arch a brow. "Done, Firecracker."

"What?" she says, like it's impossible.

"What you want, you get. I'll be back."

"Where's my mom's body?"

I swallow hard, afraid that the last little bit of heaven is over now that we're talking about her mom again, and she panics.

She places her hand over her mouth and cries.

"Please tell me you didn't throw her in the garbage, or something equally evil."

"Raina!" I snap.

"Calm down. Of course I didn't throw her in the fucking garbage. Her body is being chilled, and waiting for you to bury her wherever you see fit."

Finally, she starts breathing again, and she lowers her head and presses her face against my chest.

"I know it wasn't intentional, but I'm still so mad at you, Lorenzo. Did nobody teach you about fucking gun safety?"

I kiss her on the top of the head and tell her the truth.

"When I was six, my father taught us all gun safety, which consisted of, 'don't point unless you plan to shoot', but unfortunately misfires happen."

Raina pulls back and looks at me seriously.

"I know you think all Abruzzos are worthless, but she was important to me, Lorenzo. I want a nice burial. It's the least you can do."

I nod and admit, "It's the least I can do. Whatever you want will be done. I'll bury her in our family cemetery if you want."

She starts laughing, sounding like a crazy person.

"You're going to bury an Abruzzo in a Bonetti graveyard?"

"If it's what you want, then yes. And I don't think every Abruzzo is worthless. You aren't, and I assume your mother wasn't if she raised you."

She smiles at me, and it makes me feel like I'm a hundred feet tall, and bulletproof.

"Thank you. I'll take my lobster now."

# Chapter Thirty
## RAINA

I have to find somewhere to hide this phone because if he finds it, I'm dead. Or shocked to within an inch of my life. Like the nurse heard the panicking in my brain, she comes in with a smile on her face.

"Let's see if we can get you up and around. If you can, you're going to get to go home."

She takes out the IV, and removes the stickers on my skin from the heart monitor, and I can almost taste freedom. I know I'm leaving with Kage, whether I like it or not, but it's better than the hospital.

I grab the phone as I get off the bed, and walk to the bathroom with her.

"Looking good. I'll give you a few minutes to yourself, and come back after I talk to the doctor. There's a buzzer on the wall beside the toilet, if you need assistance."

I spot clothing on the floor beside the counter.

Kage must have brought them for me to have when I leave. As I stuff the phone into the pants pocket, the guilt is overwhelming, but I push it away. Remembering my mom and Casey makes the tightening in my chest ease. He's being nice now, saying sweet words, but it likely won't last. *One day at a time, Raina. Remember the collar, the cage, the deaths.*

I let out a cleansing breath and turn the shower on, before I retrieve the phone and make my call. She answers on the second ring.

"I'm being discharged soon, and I don't know what you want from me."

"Listen to everything you can. Find me addresses, and any incriminating information you can. Once we have what we need, we'll get you out of there, and put you in witness protection."

I nod as if she can see me.

"Alright. I have to go. I'll contact you when I have something."

I disconnect the call, turn the phone off, and put it back into my pants.

Stepping into the water, I nearly moan from how good the heat feels on my skin. I swear, a hot shower can cure almost everything wrong in life.

Almost.

My heart races when there's a knock on the door.

"Yes?" I ask nervously.

"Just checking on you, dear. Dr. Michaels said you can go home when you're done."

"Thank you. I'll be right out."

I rinse the conditioner from my hair and turn the water off.

Grabbing the towel on the rod on the outside of the shower, I dry myself off when I hear Kage outside the door.

"Firecracker, this won't work. Open the door."

"Just a second," I say, as my heart pounds, threatening to extend my hospital stay.

I get dressed quickly, and check that the shirt hangs over my jeans enough to cover the phone in my pocket. After running my fingers through my hair, I open the door to an impatient Kage, holding a bag of food in his hand.

"They said I can leave."

He shakes his head. "Not until you eat."

Pointing to the chair, Kage says, "Sit."

As I walk over and take a seat, he pulls the containers from the bags, and sets everything out for me. Lobster with butter, a baked potato, broccoli, fresh bread, and dessert.

"This is a lot of food," I giggle as I pick up the fork.

"Did you steal this? I was expecting plastic."

He shrugs his shoulders as I begin to eat.

"I did not steal it. I just told them to give it to me."

I swallow down my first bite of lobster, and shake my head at him.

"What happens if they say no?"

The smirk that develops on his lips, is both sinful and sexy as hell.

"Very few people tell me no, Firecracker."

I keep eating, but his words make me wonder if maybe I'm not the only woman in his life.

"People or women?"

He hovers over me while I eat, like I'm a prisoner at risk of escaping, which is insane because I haven't even tried. Although, I probably should.

"If you're asking if I'm fucking other women, the answer is no. I have not even considered touching another woman, since the moment I laid eyes on you. And I won't. Your sweet pussy is the only one I want."

Kage chuckles as I stop eating, and my cheeks turn bright red.

He grins proudly. "I like it when I can make your beautiful skin match the color of your hair."

I finish eating and put my fork down.

"Happy?"

"Dessert. I got your favorite."

I arch an eyebrow in question.

"How do you know what my favorite is?"

He chuckles as he points to the chocolate cake.

"Social media is amazing, baby."

"Stalker," I murmur, before I take my last bite of cake.

"Always," he smirks as the doctor walks in.

"You're free to go, but I want you to follow up with your primary doctor in two weeks. There should be no lasting complications, but I want you to have a check-up to be sure."

151

"Anything else?" Kage asks, and the doctor's response causes me to laugh.

"Maybe take a gun safety course. You guys are mafia, accidents shouldn't happen."

Obviously, Dr. Michaels wasn't told the entire truth about what happened, because it was not an accident.

Kage takes my hand and, as we walk to the elevator, I say, "Accident?"

He shrugs his shoulders as he presses the button for the bottom floor.

"We don't give reasons why people were shot. He must be assuming, since Reaper was shot and then the bullet hit you, that it was accidental, because Bones would never shoot his own brother."

Wrapping his arm around my waist, he pulls me close and murmurs in my ear.

"I can't wait to get you home, and show you how happy I am that you're alive, but first we're going to need to talk about your phone."

His words cause me to tremble. He knows. How does he know? I had it hidden the entire time. As we step outside the hospital, he turns to me.

"Hey," he says, as he places his hand on the side of my face.

"It's going to be okay. You're mine, and that means everything will be taken care of."

I glance up into his face.

"You aren't mad?"

Leaning down, he kisses me softly on the lips.

"Oh, I'm pissed, Firecracker, but not at you."

The relief spreads through me, like a fire warming me up on a frigid day. A driver pulls up, Kage opens the back door for me, and I slide in. He gets inside beside me and places his arm around my shoulders. I still can't wrap my head around the lack of death threats. Love or not, betrayal never ends well when a mafia family is involved. And I still can't for the life of me figure out how he knows.

# Chapter Thirty-One
## KAGE

I still don't understand why she thought I'd be angry for something she didn't choose. Maybe that's part of her trauma, but it's ridiculous to me. The second we get inside, I glance at my two security guys and order them, "Outside. Until further notice, you will not be inside my house."

They nod and immediately do as they're told.

Raina giggles. "What's the big guy's name?"

I scowl at her. "Tank. Why?"

He has been with me a long time, and I'd hate to lose him, but if she's attracted to him, he's gone. Or if he's made a pass at her, dead.

"He's a giant. In my head I call him Hulk, but Tank definitely fits."

I wind her long red hair around my fist and pull her to me.

"I need to be inside you."

She flashes me a look of disapproval, and I chuckle.

"If you keep fucking me without a condom, I'm going to get pregnant."

"Yeah?"

I smirk at her. "I bet you'll look stunning with my baby in your swollen belly. Fuck, Firecracker. I have never even wanted kids. You make me crave things I shouldn't."

Bending down, I place my arm behind her legs and lift her into my arms. She puts her arms around my neck, but doesn't question where I'm taking her. Having her is a need like nothing I've ever experienced. She's the fucking calm to my storm. The rain to my drought. I didn't know what my feelings for her were called. I thought it was a simple obsession, but it's more than that. Now I know I'm fucking in love with her. Do I want her to say it back?

Yes, of course I do, because then I won't have to worry about her trying to leave me, but it doesn't make me want her less. It only makes me want to show her that, yes, I do bad shit, but I'll always take care of her.

I carry her into the bedroom, set her on her feet, and stare at her. The way she pulls her bottom lip between her teeth makes me crazy.

"Get undressed."

She undoes her jeans and lays them in the corner beside the bed. I watch her, like a hawk watches its prey, as she removes her shirt and throws it on top of the jeans. She looks fucking edible standing in front of me, her long red hair hanging to her ass, and wearing nothing other than a virginal white bra, and matching panties.

Raina places her hand on her hips and glares at me.

"Is there a reason you're still wearing clothes?"

I pull my shirt over my head and throw it on the floor.

"Better?"

Her lips pull into a sexy little grin as she shakes her head.

"Getting there, but not quite."

I unzip my pants and pull them off, as she stares at the bulge in my boxer shorts.

"Dirty girl. Still not enough?"

She licks her lips slowly, like she's imagining how I taste, and I motion for her to step forward.

I reach around her back and undo her bra, pulling it down her arms, groaning when I see her perfect tits.

"Panties off."

She does as she's told, while I remove my boxers.

"On your knees, Firecracker."

I take my cock in my hand and fist it slowly, as she kneels in front of me.

"Have you done this before?"

Instantly, I regret my question, because the look in her eyes nearly kills me. Of course she did. Her fucking uncle.

154

I stroke the side of her face with my free hand.

"That didn't count. This is your first time. Next time, your hands will be tied behind your back. Start by licking my shaft."

She swirls her tongue around my balls, before running it up the underside of my cock. When she reaches the tip, and licks at it like it's a goddamn ice cream cone, I nearly lose my mind. I fist my hands in her hair.

"Suck the head, baby."

Taking the tip in her mouth, she sucks just like she was told to, and moans around me. I slide further into her mouth with a groan.

"That feels so good. I'm going to fuck your mouth now, and when I come, I want you to drink it. If you don't, I'm going to punish you."

She whimpers as I push all the way in, hitting the back of her throat, as tears spring to her eyes. Grabbing onto the outside of my thighs, she digs her nails into my flesh, while I watch my cock move in and out of her mouth.

"Fuck, yes. I knew you'd look beautiful with your lips wrapped around my cock."

I pull my hips back, and then push forward with quick thrusts, as I chase my orgasm. Every time I hit the back of her throat, it feels fucking amazing, and I know I won't last as I normally could. She squeezes her thighs together to ease the obvious throbbing of her clit, and it sends me over the edge. Moving my hands to the back of her head, I shove into her mouth one last time, and hold her in place as I shoot cum down her throat. I pull out of her mouth, and she licks her lips like she wants more.

"Stand up."

I take her face in my hands and stare at her, as I notice her hand over her heart.

"Are you in pain?"

She shakes her head no.

"The scar is repulsive."

I grab her wrist and yank it away.

"There is no part of you that's repulsive. And you won't hide anything from me."

Leaning down, I kiss her scar softly.

"This is a mark to remind me that I almost lost you. Something I'll never allow to happen again."

I slide my hands around her back, down to her ass, and lift her. She giggles, as she wraps her arms around my neck so she doesn't fall. I walk over to the bed and lie her down, before getting on the bed beside her.

Rolling over to my back, I flash her a grin.

"Sit on my face, Firecracker. Let me taste that sweet pussy."

# Chapter Thirty-Two
## RAINA

My feelings for Lorenzo are a big jumbled mess. How can you hate someone, but want them to touch you? The intensity of his gaze, the way he watches me like nothing else exists, is powerful. I keep trying to remind myself about the terrible things he has done to me. After all, that's why I agreed to give the ADA what I could. This is why I can't say no, even though I should, but I also know he wouldn't listen anyway. Lorenzo Bonetti is used to taking whatever he wants. All four Bonetti brothers are probably the same in that regard. Yet, when he tells me to sit on his face, I'm immediately wet with desire, for the tongue that does things to me I didn't know were possible.

"Sit. on. my. fucking. face. I'm starving, Firecracker."

My cheeks blush, as I stand on the bed and straddle his face. He grabs my hips and pulls me down, so I'm literally sitting on him.

He runs his fingers over the scars on my thigh, and his voice comes out sounding like he's in pain.

"No more of this, Firecracker. Nobody hurts you, not even you."

A tear rolls down my face, but he doesn't give me long to think about the past, as he pulls me down and lashes at my clit with his tongue.

I may be worried about his suffocating, but he's not, as he licks at my pussy like he can't get enough.

"So fucking good," he groans, while reaching behind me and shoving two fingers inside me. Fucking me with his fingers, as he sucks on my clit, has me ready to lose my mind with pleasure. I brace myself by placing my hands on the wall behind Kage. He glides his free hand all over my body; my thigh, stomach, and breasts. He touches me everywhere frantically, like he can't get enough.

He scissors his fingers inside me, and it's like he hit a switch that I have no control over.

"Lorenzo!"

My orgasm hits me like a freight train, spots blind my vision, and I nearly fall over from the lightheaded feeling.

Kage grabs my hips and holds me down on his face, lapping at my pussy like it's his job to get every drop.

Grabbing my waist, he lifts me off him and throws me on the bed like a rag doll, before he climbs over me and pushes my legs back. His expression is dark and almost looks like he's angry. The intensity only makes me want him more. The man I shouldn't let touch me, yet I want him. I crave him.

He slams inside me, with a sexy grunt that makes my insides pulse around his cock.

"Jesus Christ, Raina. You make me need you in a fucking visceral way. Sometimes I think if I can't fuck you, I'll die."

Leaning over me, he presses his wet lips to mine, making me taste myself on his tongue, and it makes me moan with need, as he starts to move inside me. I run my hand over the large tattoo on his chest. It looks like a heart made of barbed wire, with fragments of a skull in it.

He smirks at me like he can read my mind.

"The barbed wire is because I thought my heart was impenetrable. I wasn't even sure I had one, and then there was you."

"Lorenzo," I whisper, as the guilt crashes in on me, and a tear rolls down my cheek.

He runs his thumb through my tears and groans.

"So beautiful."

Pulling his hips back, he snaps them forward, hitting something deep inside me that makes me scream his name, as I dig my nails into his skin.

"You want to mark me, Firecracker? That's fine. I'll give you the goddamn tattoo machine, so you can mark my skin the way you have my soul."

His words are a complete contradiction to the things he's done before, yet they hit me straight in the heart.

He pinches my nipple.

"Be a good girl, and give me what I want."

"I don't think I can."

I roll my eyes at him. "It's not something I can control."

His grin is both delicious and evil.

"Such a fucking beautiful brat. When I tell you to come, you will. I promise you, you'll give me everything I want."

I'm instantly annoyed at how controlling he is, so I glare at him.

"You can't make someone come when their body is done."

He winks at me, and the butterflies swirl in my belly. I have no idea why that's so hot, but it is.

"Challenge accepted, Firecracker."

Kage changes his position slightly, and slides in and out of me, hitting my clit with his pelvis every time he does. I want to prove to him that he can't control my body, but obviously he does. Throwing my head back, I moan loudly, as my back arches off the bed.

He lowers his head and growls in my ear.

"When I tell you to fucking come, you will. Do you understand?"

I didn't, but I sure as hell do now.

"Yes."

He gets onto his knees, and digs his fingers into my ass cheeks, as he picks up his pace and fucks me hard and fast.

I watch him and take in the way his muscles flex, the mesmerizing ink on his skin on display for me, and the way his face shows pleasure as he fills me.

"Fuck," he grunts as he comes, and I have no idea how a bad man can look this beautiful.

Eventually he's going to want to discuss the ADA, and even though he said he's not mad, I'm afraid, because he must be. Nobody betrays the mafia without consequences. Somehow, when he wraps his arms around me, and moves us both to the head of the bed, I put it out of my head.

Lorenzo holds me to his chest, like he never wants to let me go, and his warmth is everything I need. His heart beats against my ear, and I already know I'm telling that ADA to go fuck herself. I was angry for what he did, but I don't want anything to happen to him. Or his brothers. Even the one that shot me.

"Lorenzo?"

"Hmm?" he hums softly.

"Not now, but will I ever be allowed any freedom? Like leaving the house?"

Moving his head, he kisses my cheek.

"Yes. If I can trust you, but you'll never go anywhere without someone. I need to know that you're safe at all times."

"Thank you," I murmur against his chest. I don't care that it's not now, and it may not even be soon, but to know that I won't be locked up here forever is enough for me.

"Go to sleep, Firecracker. I'll have a present for you in the morning."

I pop my head up. "What is it?"

He shakes his head.

"You'll see. If you're good."

# Chapter Thirty-Three

## KAGE

After she falls asleep, I climb off the bed, being sure not to wake her. I kiss her softly on the neck and she stirs, while moaning my name, but doesn't wake up. I can't help but stare at her while I get dressed. The last thing I want to do is leave her, but I need to do this.

I pull my pants on, and go into my armoire, and grab something I rarely use. A sword. It's not how I normally handle things, but special cases call for special circumstances.

Taking one last glance at Raina, I take a deep breath. Every time I look at her, I'm struck by her perfection. It's just like Bones said he felt about Athena. *Fucking breathtaking.*

I turn away from her, and head through my house so I can go to Psycho's as planned. As I head out, I stop to talk to the man Raina calls Hulk, and give him very clear instructions.

"My girl is upstairs sleeping. Nobody goes inside unless she's in danger. Perimeter check every half hour. Things will change with her here. Anything happens to her, and it's your neck on the line. Literally."

He nods like the good soldier he is.

"Understood, Boss."

I walk away from him, and get into my Range Rover with a smile on my face. Reaper is the only one of us that kills for fun. Bones, Psycho, and I don't go looking for someone to kill, just to kill them, but when we get to do it, it's fucking beautiful. We enjoy it. Especially when the person is someone who has wronged us greatly. Tonight, Leo Abruzzo is that man. When he violated Raina all through her childhood, he wounded her deeply. By hurting her, he hurt me. After I saw how she reacted to me simply mentioning her phone, I decided to let Psycho handle it. And sure enough, that's who the text message was from. The asshole who likes to touch little girls for his own sick pleasure, and is still tormenting her with his text messages. After tonight, he will not be.

I pull up to Psycho's mansion and park. His team sees me, but don't say a word. They never bother any of us. Walking around to the side door that leads to the basement, I go down the steps and enter my code to get in, while carrying my sword in my left hand.

The door closes behind me automatically, and I walk to my brother's slaughter room. He calls it an office, but that's not accurate. Nobody other than us has ever entered his 'office', and left alive. It's a slaughter room.

He points to a shaking Abruzzo in a cage.

Psycho chuckles. "It felt like it's what you would do."

And I'm interested in that, but I'm equally curious about the pretty brunette tied to his table with the muffled screams.

"Shit, brother. I didn't know you had a date tonight."

He stands beside the metal table with his favorite knife in his hand, a ka-bar with his name engraved on the blade. This woman, whoever she is, has lost a lot of blood, and I can tell he's been at it a while, because she has stitches all over her body. That is his trademark after all.

"Meet Diana. She prefers Didi, but we don't give a fuck, do we, Diana?"

She tries to say something but can't, because of the purple duct tape over her mouth.

"Purple?" I ask with a laugh.

"It's her favorite color. See, I am a nice guy."

Leo is crying in the corner, and I turn to him with a glare.

"It'll be your turn in a minute, asshole. Just wait."

Turning back to Psycho, I ask, "What did she do?"

He turns to me, pointing his bloody knife as he talks, "The ADA I told you about that's been sniffing around. This bitch is her friend, and was spying at the warehouse on 7th."

162

I shake my head in disapproval.

"Oh, Didi," I say with a smirk.

"How do you want to do this?"

He chuckles obnoxiously.

"Fine, I'll kill her so we can carry on, but I'm going to kind of miss the way she screams."

I shake my head at him.

"There will be another."

He grins with the excitement of a little kid.

"There's always more. Maybe I should be a serial killer like Reaper."

I narrow my gaze.

"You take way too long. You wouldn't get nearly enough kills."

Staring down at her, he pulls her dark brown ponytail back and looks into her eyes, as she trembles on the table.

"Goodnight, bitch. Maybe in your next life you'll be less stupid."

He slashes her throat, and the blood pours from her flesh onto the table, and eventually the floor. My brother, the psycho that he is, chuckles.

"Well, I don't think we can stitch that one up."

We walk over to the cage holding Leo. He sits shaking like a fucking leaf, in jeans that have clearly been soiled. Psycho comes over beside me, and we watch him like you might an animal in a cage. Waiting to see if they do anything exciting.

My brother looks at me with disgust on his face.

"I hope that's just piss."

I nod in agreement, but it would not be the first time someone shit their pants in Psycho's basement. Honestly, I think it's happened in all of our basements. He tries to pull his stained t-shirt down over his fat belly, but it doesn't work well.

"When I saw your text message to my girl, I was not pleased."

He shakes his head furiously.

"I didn't text nobody."

Nice use of the English language, asshole.

"Raina. She's mine, and you fucked up by ever touching her."

He holds his hands up in defense, as if he has any.

"I didn't know."

Psycho reaches through the cage, grabs him by the shirt, and pulls his face, smashing it against the bars, speaking through a clenched jaw.

"You knew she was a little girl though, right?"

My brother is as pissed as I am. The Bonetti men are not known for good deeds, but we don't fucking molest children. That's a line none of us will ever cross. There's good, bad, evil, and fucking disgusting. We are a mixture of the second two.

Psycho lets him go, and he falls to the floor with a whimper.

"I want you to know what's going to happen. No surprises."

The terror travels through him visibly as he listens to me.

"Normally, I would have kept you in a cage for weeks, you would have suffered, and eventually died from starvation. I can't do that, because Raina is at my house, and I don't want her thinking constantly about you being in the house. If I have my way, you'll never cross her mind again after today."

He cries out desperately.

"Please let me go. I swear, I'll never touch another girl."

I turn to my brother with an arched brow.

"What do you say, Psycho? Should we let him go?"

We both laugh, and Leo starts crying so hard he vomits on the floor of the cage. My brother starts screaming.

"Fucking pig. Lick it up."

Appearing to have a pair of balls for a moment, he looks at Psycho and shakes his head no.

"You're going to kill me anyway. You lick it up."

I've seen it before, so it's not surprising when Psycho snaps. He opens the door to the cage, and grabs Leo's white hair, slamming him down to the floor, which in this case is metal bars covering concrete, not very comfortable.

"Lick. It. Up."

Psycho lets go of him and stands beside me. We both stand with our heads tilted, like we are watching some new interesting discovery. It takes a lot to turn my stomach, but it's pretty fucking gross. Eventually, Psycho starts laughing and so do I, as we talk about the last thing he ever eats being his own vomit. Once he finishes, I grab him by the shirt and pull him out of the cage. I stare at his vomit covered face and shake my head.

"You really are one gross motherfucker. Now get on your knees."

He does as he's told, but whimpers like a pussy.

"You said you'd tell me, you didn't tell me."

"Right. My apologies."

I show him my sword.

"I'm going to cut your fucking head off, and present it to my girl as a gift."

He looks at me in pure shock, and it's honestly hard to keep a straight face.

"I'm romantic like that."

Glancing at Psycho, I ask, "You think this will work?"

He starts cackling like a maniac, with his hands on his knees, literally doubled over in laughter.

"No, I don't. That thing is dull as fuck. Eventually it might work, but you'll be here for the next week."

He walks to the back of the room, and presses a button, revealing a wall of blades.

Taking one off the wall, he brings it over to me. "If you're going to do it, do it right. This is why you need them custom made, Kage."

Every knife my brother has is a custom. He won't have it any other way, but he kills this way frequently, and the rest of us don't.

I take a look at it, and it's a curved sword, but it looks sharper than mine. I guess we'll see if it works as well as I want it to.

165

I look to make sure Psycho is out of the way, and swing it back, before swinging hard at Leo's neck. His head hits the floor first, followed by his body, and I stand shocked.

"Holy shit. That was fucking awesome."

My gaze moves from the sword in my hand to Leo's head on the floor.

I'm in awe as I continue staring.

"Do you know what's not awesome, Kage?"

Leo's cold, dead, pale blue eyes are wide open, as I continue looking at him. I may have to do this again, because I didn't hate that.

"When you make a fucking pact with your brother, and break it."

He jabs his blade into my thigh.

"What the fuck, Psycho?!"

My brother looks at me with pure disappointment.

"Oh, come on, Kage. You knew it was coming. Pull your pants down and sit. I'll stitch you up. If you're a good boy, I'll even give you a lollipop."

I pull my pants down, and sit on the chair near the metal table with the dead girl on it.

"Fucking asshole."

He grabs his supplies, and presses a towel down to stop the bleeding.

"I barely even got you. I told you I was going to stab you. You deserved it."

My brother is full of shit. He stabbed me deep enough to require stitches, but not so much that I'll die.

I groan more in annoyance than anything, but he's right. If there's anything we all know, it's that you don't make a bet or a pact with Psycho, unless you're willing to pay up.

# Chapter Thirty-Four
## RAINA

I wake to Kage, kissing my neck softly, and I moan as I open my eyes with a smile on my face.

"Your present is here, Firecracker. It'll start to smell if we wait too long."

My eyes pop open at his words.

"Start to smell?"

He looks at me like it's obvious, and I know what the hell he's talking about.

Kage pulls the blankets off me.

"Come on. It's in the kitchen."

I get up with a groan, and grab the bathrobe and slip it on.

"Nobody else is here?"

He grins at me, seeming excited for me to see his smelly gift.

"Just us, Firecracker."

Taking my hand, he walks me to the living room, and I scream as I jump back.

"What the fuck?"

Leo's head sits on a silver platter on top of the coffee table, his eyes fucking staring at me. I run behind Kage, as my heart pounds so hard I think I might need to go back to the hospital.

"He's dead, baby."

This is my gift? A severed head?

I peek around Kage, and see what was my uncle's head sitting there staring at me. I can't handle it. I simply can't.

"Can you close his eyes?"

He walks over and does as I asked, as I still stand stunned.

"Do you not like it?"

I laugh because it's ridiculous.

"Lorenzo, I love that you killed him for me, but you could have just told me that he was dead. I did not need proof. But thank you. Now, can we get rid of the head?"

He smiles, and it hits me right in the heart. When Kage smiles, his eyes brighten, and it's beautiful. Much better than when he's angry.

"Go upstairs. I'll take care of it and wash my hands."

I go to the bedroom and wait, while he disposes of the damn head. The part about the smell makes sense now. He comes into the bedroom and says, "Give me five minutes for a shower."

Taking a seat on the edge of the bed, I watch the news, as I roll my eyes at the television. Some things never change. This world is a dark place. And in a flash, mine gets a whole lot darker.

# Chapter Thirty-Five
## KAGE

"Raina, what the fuck is this? Why do you have another phone?"

She swallows hard, but says, "That's the one she brought me."

I open it and see there's only one contact, and one text. I read the last message.

*Anastasia:* *He doesn't love you. That's not something the Bonettis are capable of. You've helped me so far, but I need more. Don't give up.*

"Who's Anastasia?"

"The ADA," she says.

Two words that send my world into chaos.

I swallow past the bile threatening to rise in my throat.

"You've been talking to the District Attorney's office? About my family?"

She nods, with tears rolling down her face.

"You knew about this, Lorenzo. You said you wanted to talk about my phone, but never did."

I toss the phone in the sink and clench my fists.

"I knew about the text message from your uncle. Do you really think if I knew you'd betrayed me like this, that you would still be alive?"

My head is fucking spinning, and I cannot get control of my thoughts.

"This must have been really fucking entertaining for you, isn't that right, Abruzzo?"

She shakes her head. "Lorenzo, it wasn't like that."

I run a hand through my hair, nearly pulling at the roots, and I know now, I do have a fucking heart. And right now it's smashed.

"I'm a goddamn fool. I should have killed you the day I found you. I made a mistake then, but now I'll correct it."

"Lorenzo, no. I was angry. Look at the texts. I told her I wouldn't help her. I didn't want anything to happen to you, or your brothers, but especially not you."

I step closer to her and glare at her.

"Get on your fucking knees, Raina."

She gets off the bed and kneels on the floor, as I take in the woman that made a fool of me. I would've given her everything, and it pisses me off that she's still so goddamn beautiful it nearly takes my breath.

I walk over to the end table, pull out the drawer and grab the pink shock collar she wore before.

Pushing her long hair to one side, I place it around her neck, ignoring her pleas for me to listen to her.

"You were in the cage in the bedroom before, because I wanted you near me, at all times. Even if you were in there, I wanted to look at you. Now, the sight of you makes me sick, so you'll be in the basement. It's like death row. Once you end up there, you don't ever see the light of day again. You just better hope my brothers don't want to come torture you before you die."

I grab the remote for the shock collar as she sobs.

"Please, Lorenzo. Listen to me."

The truth is I couldn't hear her if I wanted to. I can't hear a damn thing beyond the screaming in my head.

I press the button on the controller twice, and she falls to the floor and shakes, while she claws at her throat, trying to stop the pain. I don't take pleasure in it, it's a shared pain. It doesn't make me feel good, but I don't have a choice. She already made the decision for me.

Knowing damn well she won't be able to walk well, I pick her up, hating it when she wraps her arms around my neck, and carry her to the basement.

She sobs into my chest, and it only makes me hate her more than I already do. I press the code to enter my basement, carry her over to the cage, and set her inside before locking it.

"I have to go tell my brothers what you've done. Don't expect to live long, Raina."

Again, she begs me to spare her life.

"Please, Lorenzo."

I narrow my gaze at her as the anger builds in my chest.

"It's *Kage*. You've lost the right to call me by my given name. Also, it's not only up to me, Raina. There's a way we handle people who do this to us. I'll spare you the details, but it will not be pleasant. You should have died twice already. Now you will."

I head to Bones' house, after telling him everybody needs to be there, including the women. This affects everyone, so they should be present when I tell them what Raina did. I brought the phone with me, in case my brother wants to see it. We need to find out who the hell this ADA is, and figure out how to handle it. Prison is not an option. It's weird to me that it's an ADA handling this, because normally they put special teams together for taking down mafia families, but it's entirely possible she's part of a bigger team.

I pull up outside my brother's house and park. Taking a deep breath, I get out of my Range Rover and make it to his door.

He stands in the doorway with an arched brow, and concern etched on his face. I knew he could tell something was very wrong, but I refused to tell him until we were all together.

"Everybody's inside already."

We walk toward my family, sitting on the couch. Bones goes over and sits by Athena, and beside her sits Bella, with Reaper beside her. And on a chair in the corner is Psycho, who looks at me with worry.

"You look like shit, brother. Everything okay?"

I shake my head.

Athena asks, "Where's Raina? You should have brought her."

I take a seat on the dark leather chair placed across from the sofa.

"I want to start by saying I'm fucking sorry. This is my doing, and I take full responsibility."

Bones eyes me warily.

"What's going on, Kage?"

I swallow past the lump in my throat.

"When Raina was in the hospital, an ADA visited her. Gave her a phone, and there's been some contact."

The entire room fills with the word 'fuck' in concert, and everybody starts asking questions over the top of each other, and again, my goddamn head spins.

Athena gets up and walks back to the kitchen, as she yells for Bella's help. Bella runs after her, as my brothers all stare at me like I've destroyed the family, and they're right, I have.

They both return with Whiskey, and glasses for all of us. I say thank you because, fuck, I need a drink right now. Or ten.

Picking up a glass, I take a long pull as Bones starts asking questions.

"First thing we need to know is what was said."

I shrug. "I wouldn't let her talk. I was pissed, but here's the cell phone."

"You haven't read them?"

I stare at the liquid in my glass as I answer him.

"No."

Psycho says, "Obviously we have to kill her."

I cringe at him, and at myself, because I still don't want to fucking kill her. If Bones says to kill her, I will not have a choice.

It's one thing to refuse to kill a woman that was simply born into a rival family. It's an entirely different situation when she's betrayed us.

Bones scrolls through the messages on the phone.

"We need to find out what was said in that hospital room, but honestly, based on these text messages they have nothing. Everybody knows we deal in drugs and weapons. That's not news. And I doubt Raina would have useful information for them at this point. They should've tried for Athena."

Psycho says, "Athena would never fucking betray us. I still say she needs to die. Sorry, brother, I know you're all warm and fucking squishy for her, but she's a liability."

Athena and Bella share a glance, like they're having a conversation the rest of us can't hear.

She looks over at Bones.

"Can I say something?"

He gazes at her softly as Psycho groans.

"Of course, Butterfly."

"The Bonetti men have a habit of taking people that maybe don't want to be taken. And I'm happy now."

She squeezes my brother's hand.

"I'm very happy, but that wasn't always the case, and I bet Bella would agree. If an ADA would've come and talked to me back then, before we were married, I might have cooperated."

Bella shakes her head.

"I definitely would have. I'm glad that didn't happen, but I hated Nico at first."

Reaper glances at Bella with an unsure expression on his face.

"But you wouldn't now?"

She giggles softly.

"I wouldn't now, Nico. Of course not. Besides, at this point my body count is getting as high as yours, so I doubt they'd help me."

Bones rises off the sofa and says, "Let's go. We need to talk to her, and," he looks at Psycho, "we are just talking tonight. This is Kage's girl. How he wants this handled will carry weight."

# Chapter Thirty-Six
## RAINA

One angry Bonetti coming at you is enough, but six is fucking terrifying. Bones stares at me with an angry expression, as he rubs his thumb over his jaw.

"Well, well, well, here we are again."

Bones and Psycho look angry. The women look like they pity me, as if they know how unpleasant my death will be, but the worst is Lorenzo. He stares at me like he can barely stomach looking at me. I miss the way he looked at me before. Like he needed me, but now I think what he said he felt for me has evaporated.

"Lorenzo, I'm sorry."

"It's Kage," he bites.

"We need to know exactly what was said in that hospital room. Leave nothing out," Bones says, with his wife behind him.

"Not much. She asked about your business. I said drugs and trafficking. She asked if I meant human trafficking, and I clarified that it was weapons, and to my knowledge, you didn't traffic humans, or deal in prostitution."

He stares at me, with eyes as black as coal. Well, really they all do, but my attention is on Bones.

"You don't know anything about my family. Why you?"

I shrug my shoulders, because I don't have much of an answer to that.

"She wanted me to try to overhear his conversations. I don't think she thought I had much, but that I could get what she wanted. I sent her a text telling her I wouldn't help."

Bones nods.

"Yeah, that you loved my brother, and would not help put him in prison. After you already spoke to her."

Kage makes a sound I've never heard from him, as he rubs his chest. I know that me saying I love him now means nothing. It's all too little too late.

"Why did you do this?" Bella asks.

"He killed my best friend, and my mother. I was angry. And given this opportunity. I didn't reach out to her, she simply showed up, and I made a mistake. The second I realized what I had done, I tried to undo it."

Kage shakes his head in disgust.

"This cannot be undone. This is something your father would've done. Once an Abruzzo, always an Abruzzo."

"We're done here. Kage, a word."

They walk to the exit, but I can just barely hear them speaking.

"I'm going to honor my wife's wishes. If you want her dead, I accept that, but you're going to need to do it. I don't think she did any real damage. However, you need to make sure she doesn't have information in the future that could be used against us."

Kage hangs his head down.

"She's a traitor."

Athena says, "Is she really, though? She was your captive."

Kage comes over to me as they all leave, and opens the door.

"Get out."

"Are you letting me go?" I gasp.

He chuckles, but there's no humor behind it.

"Well, that's what you want, right? That's what you always wanted?"

I burst into tears all over again as I step out of the cage.

"No, I don't want to go, Lorenzo. I want to be with you."

Stroking his fingers down my face, his voice comes out low, deep, and filled with pain.

"That's what I wanted too, Firecracker. Fuck, I wanted it so bad, I imagined you. I let myself believe the fantasy I concocted was real. Tell me, Raina. Do you want to live?"

"I know you think you hate me, but if you kill me, you'll never forgive yourself."

He places his hand around my throat, and shoves me against the wall, causing me to whimper when I hit my head against the concrete.

"You have one use to me now. What we had we will never have again, because I'll never fucking trust you. Take the bathrobe off."

I undo the ties on the robe and drop it to the floor.

"Turn around."

While I don't have a clue what he's doing, I do as I'm told. If I want any chance with Lorenzo, I know better than to defy him right now. There's a time to be a brat, and this is not it. Turning around, I face the wall, and he lifts my wrist, chaining me to the wall. I tilt my head back and look up because I hadn't noticed they were there. He puts my other one in the matching metal restraint, and I cry, because that's all I can do right now.

"You're my whore now, Raina. I'll fuck you whenever I want, and then leave you like this, with my cum dripping down your thighs."

He unzips his pants and I cringe. Of course I want him, but not like this.

"Lorenzo, please, I'll give you what you want, but not this way."

Grabbing my hips, he pulls my ass back and rubs his cock between my cheeks.

"These are the rules, Abruzzo. You don't talk to me. Unless you're given permission, you will not look at me. I'll take your cunt when I want it, but you have nothing to offer me. The girl I thought I loved is dead."

My heart shatters into a million pieces as he pushes inside me, and I feel like that little girl all over again. The one that learned her only worth was between her legs. He finishes inside me with a grunt and then he's gone, like he said he would be.

I rush over to the toilet, that I barely make it to with these chains, and expel everything in my stomach. After I get up, I spot Kage, watching me from the doorway. Our eyes meet, and he shakes his head and walks away.

# Chapter Thirty-Seven
## RAINA

*Two Weeks Later…*

Every day is exactly the same. He uses me for what he wants, and I vomit. There's no end in sight. I understand why he is angry, but this is too much.

I hear his voice but he isn't alone. It's a female with him, but I can't make out if it's one of the Bonetti women or not.

I glance over my shoulder and find, not only Lorenzo, but Bella staring at me. Her expression shows how horrified she is.

"Jesus, Kage," she says with a gasp.

He quickly averts his gaze.

"This is how we deal with enemies."

She shakes her head in disgust.

"You love her, you idiot. She is not the enemy. Undo her restraints."

I don't know why she's here, but I'm grateful when he removes the cuffs, and I rub my red, aching skin.

"Give us some time," Bella says.

With a sad smile, she instructs me, "Follow me. It's going to be okay, let's get you a shower."

She carries a black bag, and I walk behind her. My legs feel like Jell-o, and my stomach is nauseous. We walk into a larger bathroom and she sets the bag down. Turning the water on, she asks, "How hot do you like it?"

"Hot," I answer.

I step under the hot spray as she continues to talk to me.

"I'm sorry he's doing this."

"He's angry," I respond, like that's an excuse.

She's shuffling things around, as I wash my hair that feels like a rat's nest at this point.

"No, he's not. Not really. He's hurt, Raina. He thinks you pretended to feel something for him, but it was all to get information on his family."

I laugh bitterly. "Well, I was pretty honest with how I felt about being his captive until things started to change. And now, he hates me."

I finish washing all the dried cum off my body, and open the shower door to spot clothing on the counter. Clothing. That should not be nearly as exciting as it is. She holds something in her hand.

"I need you to pee on this."

A pregnancy test.

"I'm not pregnant. I can't be."

"Kage says you've been vomiting a lot, and that you're barely eating. We need to find out what's wrong with you because he's worried. And driving us crazy, so just pee on the stick so we can rule that out."

I nod and grab the towel to dry off.

"It's awfully insensitive to send the woman that lost a baby to find out if I'm pregnant. Not that I should be surprised."

She hands me a t-shirt, and I put it on, as she responds to my statement with a soft smile.

"I volunteered. It was obviously between Athena and I. I thought I could help the most, so here I am. Kage and Reaper aren't all that different. Neither of them know how to deal with emotions, which is why this is how he has been dealing with things. He is sick with worry about what's going on with you. I know he isn't showing you that, but it's true."

After I pull on the panties and pants, she hands me the test.

"I'll step outside. Let me know when you're done."

I stare at the test with apprehension. If I'm pregnant, then what? Is he going to force me to have an abortion? Or is he going to raise

180

my baby, while I sit chained up in the basement? Will I even be allowed to see it? All the questions in my mind have the panic setting in. Taking a deep breath, I pee on the stick. Setting it on the counter, I flush the toilet and wash my hands, as I yell to Bella that I'm done.

"Now what?" I ask when she comes back in.

"We wait."

# Chapter Thirty-Eight
## KAGE

"What the fuck are you doing, man?" Reaper asks as he narrows his gaze at me.

I roll my eyes as I pick up my drink.

"You did the same fucking thing to Bella, but for no reason. She didn't do what Raina did, and you still had her chained up. Don't judge me."

He finishes his whiskey and slams the glass down on the pool table.

"Before, dickhead. Not after I realized what she meant to me. And what are you going to do if she's pregnant?"

"I don't know," I answer, because it's all I've got.

I didn't react well to finding out she betrayed me, I know that. Emotions and I don't mix well. If she's pregnant, I'm not sure what to do, because I'll never let her go off and raise my child without me. Yet, living together raising a child won't work either, because Raina will never forgive me. Hell, I'll never forgive myself. I wanted to hurt her, make her pay a price for what she did, but I went too far. Way too fucking far, and now everything is broken beyond repair.

My brother glances at his phone.

"The test is done. Let's go find out if you're going to be a father."

We walk into the basement to find the women talking, and even laughing about something. The second Raina sees me, everything changes, like the room temperature dropped ten degrees. Her posture goes from straight to hunched over, her gaze on the floor. Bella takes her hand and squeezes it, before glaring at me.

"We are going to give you a few moments alone, and I swear to God, Kage, if you chain her up, I will choke you out myself."

Her and my brother laugh as they leave us alone. I swallow hard as I approach Raina, and she flinches away from my touch.

"Raina, before you tell me what the test says, we need to talk."

She folds her arms across her waist like she's trying to hug herself, and her eyes stay on the floor.

"Look at me."

"Are you sure you want your whore to look at you?"

Fuck.

"You are not a fucking whore. You're an example of why I hope that test is negative, because I fuck up everything I touch. I can't handle shit any other way. Torture and death is all I know."

She shakes her head, still staring at the same spot on the floor.

"When does it end, Kage? Or does it? Maybe the pain keeps going until we die."

"It ends now, Firecracker. Right fucking now."

I reach out to touch her because, fuck, I want to hold her in my arms, but again she moves away from me.

"Kill us both if you need to, but I don't want you to touch me."

My need to touch her is so real that my fingers twitch, but I know if I don't respect her words, it's over. If I have any chance of fixing this, I need to listen to her. Raina has never been treated like a human being with worth, and the things I've done to her have told her that I don't value her any more than her family did. Actions speak louder than words, and my actions have shouted that she means nothing to me, when in reality she means fucking everything.

"Yeah, I'm pregnant, Kage. Congratulations. You got your whore pregnant."

Her words are angry, but I can hear the hurt in her voice. I don't know for sure what the future holds, but I don't believe there's any coming back from what I've done.

"Firecracker."

She lifts her gaze to mine, finally, with a glare.

"It's Raina. My name is Raina. Firecracker was what a man I loved used to call me. Your used up whore is named Raina."

I clench my fist, trying to control my hand.

"You will always be my Firecracker. The woman who stole my heart with one bratty comment at a time."

The green eyes I felt drawn to are gone. No longer vibrant, but dull, lifeless, in her vacant stare. I did that.

"I'm not sure you have a heart, Kage. If you did, you couldn't have-"

She doesn't finish her sentence, Raina only shakes her head, like the words are too painful to even say out loud.

With an audible sigh, she asks, "What now?"

"Now we go upstairs."

"Back to the cage in the bedroom," she says, I think, to herself.

"Back to my bed, where you fucking belong."

She stares at me with shock, as she backs up like I hit her.

"That's not where I belong. Kage, we can't just rewind because I'm pregnant."

I run a hand through my hair, as the insanity threatens to close in on me.

"I will not fuck you until you want me to, but you will sleep in my fucking bed."

Reaper and Bella walk back in, and they both watch us with concern.

Bella is all smiles, and says, "Why don't you guys go upstairs? I'll bring Raina up in a few minutes."

My brother's girl is interesting. A pretty blonde that appears to have a bubbly personality, but will kill you in a heartbeat, if you aren't family. Her and Reaper are two nuts from the same fucking shell. I can only hope that one day Raina forgives me, the way Bella has with Reaper. As we walk out of the basement to go upstairs, my brother seems to have read my mind.

"It's going to take time."

I drag a hand down my face as I admit, "I don't know how to get through this. Through to her."

He glances at me with an arched brow, like I'm an idiot.

"You didn't break it overnight. It's going to take time to fix it. You can't force this, Kage. That's our way, I know, but this time you have to be patient, and think about her. Instead of thinking about what you need, you need to figure out what Raina needs. I suggest you figure this shit out before you bring a baby into your life."

I can't help the chuckle that erupts from me, even though what he said isn't funny.

"When the fuck did our serial killer little brother gain all this emotional intelligence?"

He grins wide.

"It's all Bella, brother. I figured out along the way that if I give her what she needs, she gives me what I want. And she's happy. Seeing your girl happy is fucking everything."

I swallow hard as the memory assaults me. That's exactly why I killed her friend, because seeing her happy, knowing it was another man that put that smile on her face, made me insane with jealousy. I want to be the one to give her that, but I don't fucking know how.

"I told her she has to sleep in my bed."

He nods in agreement.

"As she should. If you give her too much space, you'll end up living here as roommates. You don't want that."

# Chapter Thirty-Nine
## RAINA

Bella pulls the chair from across the room beside the one I'm sitting in, and takes a seat facing me.

"How are you feeling about things? About the pregnancy?"

A tear falls down my cheek, surprising me, because I wouldn't think I'd have any left by now.

"I know you'll think I'm a horrible person, but I don't want this baby. We aren't going on to live some happy ever after. I'll never forgive Lorenzo for what he has done to me. Maybe I'll always be his captive, but I don't want a child tying us together."

She takes my hand and squeezes gently.

"Athena and I have our own horror stories to tell. Neither of us started out in love with our men. The Bonetti men don't always make great choices. Their ideas of consent are blurred at best. The one thing they all share is their inability to handle emotions. Kage and Psycho both only know anger. Any other emotion that surfaces turns into rage, because they don't know how to handle anything else. Sadness, betrayal, heartbreak, it's all dealt with by violence. They don't know another way, but Kage loves you. He wants to be what you need. I'm not saying to forgive him, maybe just don't close yourself off completely. Nico and I didn't have a peaceful start. He was brutal. Call me crazy, but I can't imagine my life without him now."

"You're crazy," I say, which leads to her laughing.

"Yeah, I've heard that once or twice before. I'm going to tell Kage to give you my number. If you need anything, call me. I mean it. Anything."

I swallow hard, because looking at her causes an emotional reaction.

"I'm sorry you lost your baby. And that he sent you, of all people, to give me a pregnancy test."

Tilting her head, she smiles softly.

"None of what happened is your fault. Everybody deals with things differently, I suppose, but this is my way of getting through it. I want to help you, Raina. You may not see it now, but you're going to fall in love with your baby. One day you're going to look at Kage, and not see what he did to you, but what he does to you. I believe that, because I know you are to him what I am to Nico."

"What is that?" I ask.

She breathes, "Everything."

I still think she's crazy, and as if she can read my mind, she giggles and says, "Let's get you upstairs, before Kage comes looking for you."

We get to where the guys are, and I immediately notice the pained look in his eyes. I know he regrets what he did, but I don't think I'll ever look at him, and not hear him calling me a whore in that venomous tone. It's not the word, it's the way he said it. What he meant by it. Words are only words until the person saying them gives them meaning.

# Chapter Forty
## RAINA

Bella and Reaper leave, and suddenly I'm alone with Kage.

"Let's get you something to eat," he says.

"I'm not hungry."

He folds his arms over his chest with a narrowed gaze.

"You will eat. If not for you, for our child. Athena said soup with some crackers would be good, with ginger ale."

I give up the fight and agree, because I know he's right. For the baby, I need to eat. I'm still trying to wrap my head around the fact that I'm not only having a child, but with Kage. My captor, my tormentor, and the love of my life. I'm angry with the things he did to me, the words he spoke, but because I'm an idiot, my feelings haven't changed for him. He doesn't need to know that, though.

Following him into the kitchen, I stand near the island as he opens a can of soup, and heats it on the stove.

"I'll have the chef make you homemade soup tomorrow."

He motions to the chair, and I take a seat while he opens the refrigerator, grabs a ginger ale, and hands it to me after opening it.

"Thank you."

Kage goes over to the stove, pours my soup into a bowl and brings it to me, and I take a mouthful.

"Crackers," he says out loud to himself, and brings them over to me.

Taking a seat across from me, he watches me, like me eating is somehow fascinating.

"Raina, I'm fucked up, okay, but I'm sorry for what I did to you. It wasn't right and I know that. Fuck, I knew it while I was doing it, but I couldn't control myself. The rage took hold of me, like it did the day with your friend, and I did and said things I can't take back. Somehow, I'm going to fix this."

I swallow a bite of my cracker and glance at him. His face shows that he means what he says, but I don't trust it. I don't trust him.

"And the next time I make you angry? Will it be the cage or the chains? Or will you just hold me down while you rape me?"

Kage flinches like I hit him, but recovers quickly.

"I deserve that."

Taking a spoonful of my soup, I swallow, and say, "So I'm supposed to believe you're a good guy now?"

He chuckles, with amusement dancing in his eyes, and I hate how much I like it.

"No, Firecracker. I'm not a good guy. I never have been and never will be, but I want to be good to you. I don't want to lose you. I'll be what you need me to be."

Setting my spoon in the bowl, I flash him a sad look as I shake my head. This is impossible, and he has to know that deep down.

"You are who you are, Kage. A tiger can't change its stripes. You can't lose me, when I'm not allowed to leave."

He bristles at my words, but doesn't say anything because he knows I'm right. I'm not completely blind, I know I brought the anger on myself. He had every right to be upset, but he went too far. His actions were not what a man does when he loves a woman. It reminded me far too much of my family, and I don't know how I'm supposed to erase those memories from my mind.

"Let's get you up to bed."

I rise from the chair, and he moves to put his arm around me, and then quickly retracts it. We walk to the bedroom in heavy silence. I'm heartbroken by what he did, but I can also feel his pain. I know he regrets it, but why should his feelings matter more than mine? I'm tired of being second rate to everyone around me. That's what hurts the most because, before this, Kage gave me something I had never had. He looked at me like I mattered. Then, suddenly, I was

190

downgraded to a whore. It's not that he had sex with me, because I would've given it to him willingly. It was the way he took it. The way he took me from behind, so he didn't have to look at me. The way he called me by my family's last name. The disgust, the hatred. No, I can't forget that.

I get into bed, and of course he gets in beside me, so I turn to my side, giving him my back.

"This is not going to work, Kage. I'll never forgive you. I don't want to. Find somebody else to fuck, and leave me alone."

He leans his head down and inhales the scent of my neck, coming close but not touching me.

"I don't want anyone else, Firecracker. You're still mine, and I'm still yours. If it takes a thousand years, I'll fix this."

I roll my eyes and snort laugh.

"Are you a vampire now? If not, I don't think you'll be alive in a thousand years."

He strokes his fingers down my arm as I freeze.

"I'm not going to fuck you, but I need to touch you."

"I hate you."

His last words before I fall asleep crash into my chest, and I feel like I've been shot all over again.

"Not as much as I hate myself. There is no way you could hate me that much."

I fall asleep with Kage on the other side of the bed, but somehow, I wake up in his arms. My face is pressed to his chest, with his arms around me, holding me close. Trying to push him away makes him hold me tighter, and I hit his chest.

"Let me go, or I'll puke all over you."

191

His smirk is far more annoying than delicious, as my stomach rumbles.

He lets me go and says, "Exchanging bodily fluids with you is one of my favorite activities."

"Don't be gross."

I jump off the bed and race to the bathroom, to get rid of the small amount of food in my system.

As I'm kneeling in front of the toilet, Kage kneels beside me and pulls my hair back.

"Kage, go away. You don't need to watch this."

He kisses the side of my head sweetly.

"I'm going to be here for everything, Firecracker."

I vomit until there's nothing left.

Wiping my mouth with the towel, that somehow appeared out of nowhere, I ask, "Yeah? Are you coming to see the gynecologist too?"

He presses his hand to the side of my face with a gentle touch.

"Yes, Bones is scheduling an appointment with Athena's doctor since she's a female."

"A female?"

He chuckles like it's obvious why, and lifts me off the floor.

"Yes, Firecracker, because I don't want to kill our baby's doctor."

I'm almost glad to hear him say that, because it's the first true Kage comment since he found out I was pregnant. He has been nice, which is simply confusing, because that's not the man I know.

# Chapter Forty-One
## KAGE

*Two Weeks Later…*

"I got you some maternity clothes. Get dressed, because I'm taking you somewhere."

Her expression turns from surprise to amusement, and I have no idea what I did, but I decide it must've been good, when I'm rewarded with her genuine laughter.

"I'm barely pregnant. I don't need maternity clothes."

Alright, I'll admit it. I barely know anything about women in general, and I know nothing about the pregnant ones.

"Well, you have them now. If you need anything else, please tell me. Now get ready."

"Where are we going?"

I can't help the goofy fucking grin that takes over my face as I stare at her, actually looking into my eyes. Fucking progress.

"On a date."

Raina goes for a serious expression, but it turns into laughter that I think melts my fucking black heart.

"I think you're supposed to do that before knocking the woman up."

As if she spots the hope in my gaze, she takes it away.

"I mean, yes, sir. Your captive will get ready as instructed."

Fuck. I want to spank her beautiful ass when she says shit like that, but I know better.

I take a deep breath to try to talk my cock into chilling the fuck out, and walk to the door.

"I'll wait downstairs."

My brothers are off killing an employee. Yet another fucking asshole that thinks stealing from the Bonettis is a good plan. They never learn. Bones said they could handle it without me, when I told him my plans for Raina. I said thank you, to which he responded, 'don't fuck it up'. The problem is I always fuck it up, especially with her. I have fucked a lot of women, but I've dated none. I'm still not sure what they want, so I thought long and hard about Raina specifically. Bella told me she had a flower garden at her home with her parents. So we'll start with that, and hopefully I figure out the rest as I go. Bella, Athena, and Raina have started a group chat on their phones, and they've gotten to know each other well. I'm not allowed to know exactly what's said, but Bella did tell me that, more than anything, Raina wants to be treated like she matters.

Well, fuck, that should be easy, because there's nothing, and no one, that matters more than she does.

I turn around and find her staring at me, with a blush to her beautiful pale cheeks, looking fucking stunning. She's wearing a white sundress, now that it's getting warmer, and her hair is partially up, showing off her beautiful neck. Her makeup is minimal, which is exactly how I prefer it.

"I'm ready, Master."

Rubbing at my temples, I groan, because she's turning me into my fucking always irritated brother.

"I'm trying really hard to go at your pace, Firecracker. Every time you run that smart mouth, I want to either fill it with my cock, or bend you over and spank your ass, until your skin matches your beautiful hair. As we both know, my control is rather lacking with you, so maybe behave."

She tilts her head to the side, as her lips turn up into a devious little grin.

"Ahh, there he is. I was very concerned."

"Concerned?" I repeat her word, not knowing what she's talking about.

Raina pulls her bottom lip between her teeth before she smiles, and fuck, it nearly knocks me over.

"I was getting ready to call Mulder and Scully."

Who and who? What the fuck is she talking about?

She starts laughing and, while I know it's at my expense, I don't mind it.

"From the X-Files. I was worried the aliens came and stole you, and put some Kage imposter in your place."

"Still here," I say as I file away information to look into later. I need to find out about this X-Files, because I still genuinely don't know what the hell she's talking about. And aliens?

I shake my head in confusion, but let it go.

"Ready?"

Reaching out my hand, she takes it, and I pull her hand up to my lips and kiss it softly.

We walk outside and Tank has my car sitting near the entrance as instructed.

"Hey, Hulk," she says, and he blushes and turns away instantly.

I narrow my gaze at her.

"I said, behave. How the fuck you have my giant security guy blushing like a goddamn fourth grader, I don't know. Unless you want to see another head on the coffee table, you should do as you're told."

I close her door after she gets into my Spyder, walk around to the other side, and get in.

"Are you trying to make me lose control?" I ask as I drive off the property.

She glances at me before turning her gaze out the window.

"No. Maybe I'm curious how far you'll take this good guy act, Kage. This personality change is not what I expected."

Raina is quiet for a minute before whispering, "Or what I wanted."

And just like that, my control snaps like a fucking twig.

I pull the car over and put it in park.

"I'm trying, Raina. What the fuck do you want from me?"

She glares at me in frustration, opens the door, and gets out of the car. I scramble out after her, because I don't know what's happening. My heart races, as I wonder if she's trying to run from me.

"Tell me. What do you want? I'm trying real hard to figure it out, but I'm obviously missing something."

Raina turns to me, and places her hands on her hips.

"I want it to be real, Lorenzo."

She said my name, and suddenly I can barely fucking breathe.

"My problem wasn't the man you are. I want a man that will take me when he wants me. Just not chained up, and saying I'm nothing but his whore. Don't you get that? Oh, and maybe not a shock collar, because really, that's not my kink."

Stepping over to her, I take her face in my hands and tilt her head back.

"You were never my whore. Even when I said it, I knew I was a liar."

I slide my hands from her face to the back of her neck, and hold her in place, as I thoroughly enjoy the way her breathing increases to nearly a pant. My eyes drop to her lips, as I crave the softness. She may push me away, but I have to taste her again.

Pressing my lips to hers, I kiss her slowly and she seems stunned at first, but then kisses me back. She reaches her hands up and grips my shoulders, as I push my tongue into her mouth. I break our kiss by pulling her hair, and run my tongue all over her neck. Fuck, I missed the taste of her skin. It's sweet, and smells almost like a combination of fruit and flowers.

"I said I would wait until you told me you wanted me, but I can't. I need you, Firecracker."

Lifting her into my arms, I carry her back to the car and lay her on the hood.

I unzip my pants and she looks around us, as if she's afraid someone might see us, but right now I don't care.

Pushing her dress up, I grab her thighs and pull her down, so she's at the right angle, and pull her panties to the side.

"If you don't want this, now would be the time to tell me."

She doesn't respond, so I push inside her with a groan. Fuck. Raina always feels fucking amazing, but this is better than before.

"Lorenzo," she whimpers as I move inside her, and it's like music to my fucking ears. Raina wraps her arms around my neck, and legs around my waist, as she runs her fingers through my hair.

"Finally," she moans.

I pinch her nipple through her dress, as she tilts her head back, and her pussy clenches around my cock, making me groan.

"Do that again."

Her lips pull up into a seductive grin.

"Are you making me do all the work?"

Leaning down, I pull her bottom lip between my teeth with a growl.

"Am I not fucking you good enough, Firecracker?"

I pick up my pace and rail her, as she screams my name.

"That's my girl. Taking my cock like it was fucking made for you."

She looks gorgeous on the hood of my car. There's something about the way her bright red hair looks against the black paint, the white dress pulled over her hips, and her green eyes blazing with desire.

Her eyes roll back into her head as she cries out again, with my name falling from her lips. The second I found her trying to hide from me, I knew I wanted her. It wasn't just because she's beautiful, although she is. It was more than that, the fire in her gaze. One look and I knew my thought that I craved submission was a fucking lie. What I crave is her. My pretty little firecracker.

197

# Chapter Forty-Two
## RAINA

We pull into a parking lot and I gasp.

"No fucking way."

Kage glances at me with a smirk on his lips.

"Yes fucking way."

I open the door and jump out before he turns the car off, and get scolded immediately.

"You had to wait thirty seconds. In the future, you'll wait for me to open your door."

I whine like a two year-old, "But it's the World of Flowers, Lorenzo. The World of Flowers!"

It's the largest flower showcase in the world. You can buy fresh flowers, or you can get seeds to plant your own, and this place has been a dream of mine, but my father never let me go.

*'I'm not sending a driver all the way out there, when we have flowers here, Raina.'*

"How did you know?"

Lorenzo walks over to me and wraps his arm around my waist, pulling me in close to him.

"I didn't. Bella told me about your garden at your father's house, but I didn't know about this place. Athena found it on google."

"I'm so excited," I squeal, probably sounding like a pig, but he doesn't seem to mind. He kisses me on the cheek, and we start walking to the entrance.

We walk under the huge sign above our heads, and I try to take off to look at all the flowers, but he pulls my hand back. "You'll stay with me so I know you're safe, Raina. Not only do you come from the family you came from, you're with a Bonetti now. That means danger. I promise we'll see everything there is to see."

I look up at him and nod.

"I know. I'm sorry."

We walk through the rows and rows of flowers, and he whispers in my ear when he catches me staring at my favorite flower.

"Get whatever seeds you want for your own garden at home."

I first started gardening when I was eleven years old as an escape. We all have our way of getting through things. Some people read, others listen to music, but gardening was my out. I would spend hours in the garden, making everything perfect. It wasn't just the flowers though, it was the sun, the open space. At least until my father started to bring women to the basement to torture them. He always had some reason for it, but really I think he was just a violent man getting his rocks off. I was twelve the first time I saw him raping a woman. That's an image that imprints on your soul.

"Firecracker?"

I shake my head, clearing my thoughts, and glance up into Lorenzo's waiting gaze.

"Sorry. What?"

"What's going on?" He asks, his eyes narrowing at me with concern.

"Nothing. I was just thinking about my father, and when I started gardening. I'm okay."

He kisses me on the forehead, as the lady selling the flowers squeals, saying something about young love.

"I was saying, you can have a garden at home. We have tons of land, and space will not be an issue. Whatever you want to plant, get the seeds, and you can plant them."

"Thank you."

I pick up four packets of seeds for roses, because they're my favorite, and Kage wanders off a few feet from me, and stares at a flower in awe. Moving over to him, as he talks to the lady behind the table, I listen as she explains the flower to him.

"These are imported from Oregon. They are a member of the Asparagus family. The flowers hang in clusters, giving off the appearance of a firecracker."

"Fascinating," he says, and I try to hide my laughter.

"I'll take a dozen. No, make that two dozen."

She hands him the flowers, and he turns to me with a grin.

"Hmm, Lorenzo Bonetti, a flower guy? I didn't see it."

"It's called a firecracker, it had to happen."

We walk through this place, as Lorenzo carries my now three bags, and the two dozen flowers he just had to have, and it puts a strange feeling in my chest. This tough mafia guy is doing all these things for me. I smile like an idiot, and notice him staring at me.

"What?"

He shakes his head.

"Nothing. I'm realizing that Reaper was right. Seeing you happy is everything."

He takes my hand in his, we walk to the car, and he chuckles.

"Your phone keeps going off."

I slide into the car and grab my phone, knowing it's my group chat with the girls. Lorenzo gets in the car and starts driving.

*Athena: Well, is it everything?*

*Me: More.*

*Bella: Did you get flowers?*

*Me: So many. And he found firecrackers and bought two dozen.*

*Athena: Firecrackers? The flower? How sweet is that?*

*Bella: I expect pictures.*

201

**Me:** *What news?*

**Bella:** *We set a date for the wedding. I hope you don't have plans next weekend.*

**Me:** *What? I'm invited?*

**Bella:** *I'm literally rolling my eyes at you. Obviously.*

I glance at Kage and ask, "Did you know Bella and Reaper are getting married next weekend?"

He laughs as he merges onto the highway.

"He's my brother. Of course I knew."

I scowl at him for not telling me, but he quickly diffuses it.

"Bella wanted to tell you, so I was strictly forbidden from saying anything."

**Me:** *I'm so excited! Thank you for including me.*

**Bella:** *Rolling my eyes again. I would've been more likely to include you than Kage.*

I giggle louder than I meant to, and he looks at me with curiosity.

"She likes me better than you."

He takes my hand and kisses my knuckles softly.

"Of course she does. Anybody would."

"Where are we going now?"

"Another surprise, Firecracker."

# Chapter Forty-Three
## KAGE

Happy Raina is like a goddamn drug, and I'm addicted to it.

She has spent most of her life separated from society. Her only friend was Casey, and while I don't totally regret it, I took him from her. I am never going to accept her being in another man's arms the way she was that day, but I do want her to be happy. I'm glad that she has developed a friendship with my brothers' girls. Not only is it good for her, but I like that she's slowly becoming part of my family. Psycho makes the odd comment about his feelings. He thinks I should've killed her, and I understand why. My oldest brother has never had warm feelings for a woman. I think you have to experience it to understand it. It wasn't long ago that I thought both Bones and Reaper had gone insane. Now I get it. Unfortunately for Psycho, I'm not sure he'll ever have that in his life. Hell, what kind of woman could keep up with him? Anybody that signs up to be sliced, diced, and stitched up on a regular basis, is probably scarier than Bella.

I pull up to Bones' house and she gawks at me.

"Is Athena here? Please tell me Athena is here?"

"Yeah, baby. Athena is here," I say with a grin.

She taps her feet with happiness, and I can see how much she wants to jump out, but she stays put. I get out, walk around to her side, and open the door for her.

"Good girl," I say, as I kiss her just below her earlobe, and she moans. Every fucking time I kiss her there, she moans deliciously.

As we are walking up the steps, she stops, and I can see the panic dancing in her eyes.

"Is Psycho here?"

Placing my finger and thumb on her chin, I lift her gaze to mine.

"Listen to me, Firecracker. I swear to you, my brother will not touch you. I won't allow it. Bones won't allow it, and Reaper won't allow it. Also, if I had to put money on it, I bet Bella could kick his ass, and we both know she wouldn't allow it."

She giggles as she visibly relaxes.

"That's a fight I'd pay money to see."

I don't want her to kill him, but if he keeps talking shit about my girl like he has been, I'm down to see him get his ass handed to him.

Athena opens the door, with a scream that pierces my eardrums.

"What are you doing here?" She asks, and then takes Raina's hand and yanks her from me, while my brother stands beside her, shaking his head.

Bones speaks low, as we follow our women into the living room.

"Psycho is wound up, so maybe keep an eye on things."

"About what?" I ask.

He stops walking, so I do the same, while keeping my eyes on Raina the entire time.

"The ADA was here about an hour ago. Psycho wasn't here yet, but I told him about it, and he's been going on about it ever since."

"Something to worry about?"

Bones looks over at Athena, before turning back to me.

"I don't think so. I really don't think they have any actual evidence. She's young, and trying to make a name for herself. And taking down the Bonettis would accomplish that. I'm suggesting for now we concentrate on legitimate businesses, and have our guys handling the other shit. Ones we can fucking trust."

By trust, he means ones that would gladly take a lifetime prison sentence, rather than piss off the Bonetti Brothers.

He glances at Raina before asking, "Does she know about *Kages*?"

I shake my head no, and he chuckles.

"That's probably a conversation you want to have, before she finds out by other means."

Bones is not wrong. If she finds out I own a club, with women dancing half naked in cages, she may not be pleased.

"Let's grab a drink."

As we walk toward the kitchen, he yells, "Psycho, get in here."

Neither of us think he would do anything to Raina, but we aren't taking chances.

"Where are my bitches?" Bella yells, as her and Reaper walk through the door, causing Bones to shake his head.

We can hear the women carrying on in the living room, as Bones pours us all a drink.

"When are we going to meet your woman?" I ask Psycho, and am instantly rewarded with a glare.

"Fuck you. I'm not doing this pussy whipped shit you all are."

Reaper walks in just then.

"That's a disappointment, man. I was thinking, we all nickname our girls; Bones has Butterfly. I have Living Dead Girl. Kage, Firecracker. Yours could be Stitch."

Bones laughs first, and Psycho looks at him and says, "Asshole."

Both Reaper and I wait for it.

"How many times have I told you not to call me that?"

"Too fucking many," I say under my breath.

As they stare each other down, and I wonder if they're actually going to fight, Bella walks in.

"Alright, boys, cut it out."

She kisses Reaper and beams at him, before turning and leaving the kitchen.

I turn to my brother and ask, "How is she?"

The pain in his eyes is raw, and right there on display for all of us.

"I don't know. She seems fine most of the time, but sometimes I hear her crying in the bathroom."

"She has been through a lot," Bones says, and we all nod in agreement, but it's Psycho that surprises me.

"I don't think you ever get over losing a child, regardless of how it happens. For it to happen so violently, brutally, fuck, I wish we could kill those fuckers all over again."

He raises an eyebrow at Bones.

"You should've let me do it my way."

Bones smirks at Psycho. "They'd still be alive."

Pressing the end of his blade into the tip of his finger, Psycho says, "Are we going to talk about the elephant in the room?"

We all look at him like we don't know what he's talking about, which earns us a glare.

"Your girl, Kage. She's the fucking elephant."

Slamming my fist down on the island, I roar, "We have talked about this."

Psycho shakes his head, narrowing his gaze at me, as he says, "Make me understand. Never before have we let someone live that betrayed us. Fucking never."

He stares at Bones with something that almost looks like hatred, even though I know better.

"Dad wouldn't have allowed this. Kage finds a pussy he wants to fuck, and we all turn a blind eye? I don't fucking understand."

Bones speaks calmly, but in a tone that leaves no room for misinterpretation.

"Maybe not, but there are things he allowed that are revolting. I gave Kage the choice in dealing with her, because she did not cause harm. She did not give more than they already knew. My decision is final, Psycho. I do not want to hear another word about this. Raina is pregnant with Kage's child, and that means she's one of us. It's time to let it go."

# Chapter Forty-Four
## RAINA

Athena points at her phone.

I glance at Bella and she mouths 'phone' to me, so I get mine out, although I have no idea what they're up to.

I notice a message in our group chat, so I open it.

*Athena: Trust me, Luca is listening, he's always listening.*

*Bella: He's annoying like that.*

*Me: Okay. So what's up?*

*Athena: How's the sex?*

*Me: What?*

Bella giggles beside me trying hard to be quiet.

*Bella: Please don't say you aren't getting the 'D'.*

Oh my God.

*Me: Yes?*

*Athena: Details, woman. Bella and I are in a disagreement over which Bonetti brother has the biggest dick.*

She holds up her arm and then begins to type.

*Athena: Bigger or smaller than my forearm?*

*Me: Is this a trick question?*

*Bella: Nope. Bigger or smaller?*

Jesus, he's not a goddamn elephant.

*Me: Smaller.*

*Athena: Bigger or smaller than a coke can?*

*Me: Bigger?*

*Bella: Are we talking girth or length?*

A growl, sounding like the voice of God, booms, and we all turn to find Bones narrowing his gaze at her.

"Butterfly."

Of course the other brothers come out of the kitchen, curious what's going on, and I am pretty sure I visibly shrink.

"Our women apparently want to know which of us has the bigger dick."

Psycho laughs in a way that I think is rare for him.

"Definitely me. I'm happy to show and tell, ladies."

Reaper, Kage, and Bones all turn toward him with matching scowls.

"Fuck off," they say in unison, and it's funny how alike those grumpy faces are. All three of them have a chiseled jawline that looks like the others'. Psycho, I couldn't tell you, because I look at him as little as possible.

"So, Raina. Talk to any prosecutors lately?"

And that's why.

Bones orders him to stop, and he does, for the most part. Still, he spends the majority of the evening watching me, like at any minute I'm going to destroy his entire world. I do understand why he's worried. He doesn't trust me, and I don't think trust comes easily to any of these men.

"Mom is coming over tomorrow," Kage says.

He had mentioned that she wanted to come for a visit, but I didn't know it was a done deal.

Athena smiles at me.

"You're going to love her."

I turn to Lorenzo and ask the obvious question.

"Does she know my last name?"

He kisses me on the cheek and whispers in my ear, "She does, and I promise you, it won't matter to her. My dad would've cared, but my mom does not."

Bella rolls her eyes, cuddling up to Reaper when he sits beside her.

"As long as you're a fan of her chocolate cake she'll love you."

Kage grins at me, because he knows how I feel about chocolate cake.

I wonder about his words. His mom will love me? What about him? He said he loved me before everything happened, but not since then. I can't help but worry that he doesn't feel the same, and is with me because of the baby.

"It has been a long day for Raina. We're going to head out," Kage announces, and I'm exhausted, so I'm kind of glad, but also sad to leave my new friends.

Sharing the sentiment, Bella and Athena jump up and hug me.

Athena says, "I'll message you on the group chat."

Bones stares at her with a smirk.

"There will be consequences."

Athena smiles wide, and I can't help but laugh as she says, "I'm getting spanked."

"Butterfly," Bones warns, but it only makes us laugh harder.

"Come on, Firecracker."

Kage takes my hand and walks me out, leaving the loud voices behind.

# Chapter Forty-Five
## KAGE

Raina was quiet on the drive back to our house, and now even more still. I watch her go into the restroom and get ready for bed. I slip under the sheets, after I strip down to my boxers, and wait. She finally comes out, and as I suspected, something is wrong. Her eyes are sad as she gets in the bed beside me.

"Goodnight," she says and then turns over, leaving a space between us that I'm not going to tolerate.

I place my arm around her waist and pull her against me, pressing my lips against her neck.

"Firecracker."

"Don't," she whispers.

"You can face me, or lay the way you are, but you will tell me what the fuck is going on in that pretty head of yours."

She sighs audibly before speaking.

"If I hadn't gotten pregnant, would we be together?"

"What?" I ask, thoroughly confused.

"Are we together because of the baby? Is that all we are?"

Sliding my arm underneath her, I turn her so she's facing me, and spot the tear on her cheek.

"Why are you asking this? Am I not making you happy?"

She doesn't answer whether or not she's happy. Instead, she says, "We weren't in a very good place when we found out I was pregnant. I was chained naked in your basement, Lorenzo."

I push the hair out of her face and kiss her tears softly.

"It wasn't the baby that snapped me the fuck out of my insanity. It was you. I was terrified, Firecracker. You were so sick, and wouldn't eat. I thought I was losing you, and that's when I realized you were still mine."

Raina closes her eyes, as if it's too hard to look at me.

"You said you loved me before all that happened. Either I broke what you once felt for me, or you never truly felt that way about me."

My chest squeezes with the realization that this is what's been going on in her brain. I haven't said it, but not because I don't feel that way. Fuck.

"Am I happy that you're pregnant with my child?"

Her eyes pop open, and she stares back into my eyes.

"Fuck, yes, I am, Firecracker. If you weren't pregnant, it wouldn't change things between us. I don't know why I didn't say it, but I've thought it a million times."

"You have?" She whispers softly.

I grin at her.

"Every time you smile at me, every smart ass comment that comes out of your beautiful mouth, when I watch you sleep, all the fucking time, Firecracker."

Stroking my fingers down her arm, I watch her as goosebumps develop beneath my touch.

"You haven't said it either."

A moan escapes from her, as I rub my thumb over her nipples, one and then the other.

"I was afraid you'd say you didn't love me."

This woman. I'm not a touchy feely guy with anyone other than her. I have worn my heart on my sleeve for her, only for her.

Rolling her to her back, I climb over her while she stares at me, and I know exactly what she needs.

"You don't know how I feel about you, Firecracker?"

I stroke my fingers down her throat, feeling her heart rate increase.

"I love you, Raina. With every fucking beat of my heart, but it's so much more than that. I'm fucking obsessed with you. Every time I'm away from you, it's like I'm missing a vital part of my body.

212

When you were sick, I experienced pure terror. So, yeah, I love you, but those words don't even seem powerful enough to describe what I feel for you."

"Lorenzo," she whispers, as she runs her fingers through my hair, "I love you."

I flip us both over so she's on top of me, and I pinch her nipple, immediately eliciting a moan from her sweet lips.

She sits up on top of me, her wet pussy seated just above my boxers as she wiggles slightly, aching for that friction she loves so much.

"Do you want something, Firecracker? You look very needy right now."

She pulls her bottom lip between her teeth, and gives me a sexy nod.

I run my tongue along my lower lip as I stare at her. She's stunning, sitting on top of me naked, her body craving me the way mine craves hers. Her full tits catch my attention with pebbled nipples, and my gaze travels every inch visible to me, as I try to devour her with my eyes.

"If you want it, take it."

She has come out of her shell sexually, but she still holds herself back unless I initiate it.

"My body is as much yours as yours is mine. You do not need permission, you do not have to wait for me to touch you. If you want it, take it."

Leaning over me, she places her hands on the mattress on either side of my head.

"I want to taste you everywhere."

She presses her lips to my neck, alternating between soft kisses and licks of my skin. Raina moves so her pussy is on top of my cock, as she drags her tongue along the barbed wire heart on my chest, causing me to dig my fingers into her ass cheeks. It's taking

213

everything in me to not take control of this, and slam my cock inside her like I want to.

Continuing her downward descent, she flicks her tongue over the indentations of my abs. My cock is straining against my boxers, possibly harder than it's ever been, and then she moves back up, kissing the skull and rose tattoos on one of my arms, before moving to the other.

Moving down my body again, she pulls my boxers down and grabs my now free cock, and strokes it slowly.

Raina looks fucking gorgeous straddling my thighs, stroking my length, with her long wavy red hair hanging down to her ass, watching me with a gaze I'm trapped in. I never wanted to be like either of my two brothers, addicted to a woman. This is everything I've ever tried to avoid, yet now I can't fucking figure out how I ever lived without it. Without her.

"You're killing me, Firecracker."

She gazes at me with a sexy little smirk.

"Do you want something, Lorenzo? You look very needy. If you need something, take it."

*Fucking brat.*

# Chapter Forty-Six
## RAINA

Lorenzo places his hands under my arms, pulls me up and flips me over to my back, climbing over me with a growl.

"If I need it, take it? Well, I fucking need it."

He slides one side of his boxers down, and then the other, before kicking them to the end of the bed.

Kneeling on the bed in front of me, he spreads my legs, and stares between them with a heated expression.

"So wet. So desperate to be filled."

I whimper, as he gazes at me like he might eat me alive, and I hope he does.

He chuckles softly.

"I think it's time for you to learn what happens when you misbehave like a little brat, Firecracker."

"What?" I ask, and he slaps my pussy.

I yelp loudly, which is only met with his laughter.

"This is what happens when you taunt me."

He slaps me again and I scream, but I'm not sure if it's the sting, or the way my clit is pulsing with need.

"You want to think about my brothers' dicks?"

Again he slaps my pussy, but harder than before.

"Lorenzo!"

"Am I correct to believe that won't happen again?"

I gasp out, "Yes. Never."

He smirks at me.

"Good, because I guarantee mine is the biggest, the best, and the only fucking cock that will ever touch you."

I don't bother telling him that it wasn't even me who started that debate. That was Athena. She's a bad influence, and I intend to tell her exactly that.

"You're my filthy slut. Mine and mine alone."

My eyes roll back into my head at his words, as a whimper slips out of me.

He runs his tongue over his bottom lip, knowing it drives me crazy.

"You like that, Firecracker. Do you like it when I call you my slut?"

"Yes," I admit in a near scream, "Please, Lorenzo, please."

He slides his fingers up my slit as he groans.

"Such a good little slut, begging so prettily for me."

He pushes inside me, sliding his arms under my back, and lifts me as he sits back on his feet. I wrap my arms around his neck, as he moves me up and down his cock.

Grabbing my hair, he pulls my head back and slams his lips to mine, with a kiss that is both dominating and possessive. He tilts my head slightly, sliding his tongue against mine while he fucks me. My breasts are pressed against his skin, his arms around my back, as we move as one body. I don't know how I expected my life to turn out, but it wasn't this.

My body trembles against his, and he breaks our kiss with a sexy groan.

"That's my girl. Give me your pleasure."

Every word, every touch, every thrust inside me, sends me falling head first into an orgasm that takes complete control of my body, just like he does. It starts as tiny sparks move through my core, until I'm screaming in ecstasy but never wanting it to end.

"Lorenzo!" I cry out as I fall apart.

He lifts me off him and turns me over.

"On your knees."

Spreading my ass cheeks, he swipes his tongue over my back hole, and I instantly freeze.

"Shhh," he murmurs, "Do you trust me, baby? Do you know I am not going to hurt you?"

"Yes," I say, my voice coming out shaky, but I do know what he asked is true. I know in the depths of my soul that Lorenzo won't do anything to hurt me.

"Good girl. I own all of you, Raina. Including this beautiful ass. I promise, we'll take it slow. I'll make you feel so fucking good, you'll beg for it next time."

He swirls the tip of his tongue around the opening, and I whimper. It's different than anything else he has done to me. Everything in me says to not like it, because when Leo touched me there, it hurt so bad I wanted to die.

Pushing the tip of his tongue inside me, he swirls it around in circles, as I dig my fingers into the mattress.

"Lorenzo," I whimper, needing more.

He pushes his tongue all the way inside me, and I push back against him with a loud moan.

Pulling his tongue out, he says, "I'm going to insert a finger. Rub your clit for me."

I freeze again as he rubs his finger along the rim.

"Trust me, Firecracker. Trust that I'm going to make you feel so good, that you're going to scream louder than you ever have."

He pushes his finger in, and I bury my face into the mattress as I clench down on his finger.

"Relax, baby. Rub that clit for me."

I do as he says, and he pushes his finger in further, as I rub circles on my clit, like he does when he touches me. The sensation is overwhelming, but pleasurable after a few minutes.

"That's it, baby. You're such a fucking good girl. Keep playing with your pussy. I'm going to insert a second finger, and then you're going to come for me."

Once he has two fingers inside me, I feel so full, but can't stop myself from pushing back against his fingers.

"Lorenzo."

"That's my girl. Give it to me."

A combination of his words, voice, and what he's doing to me, sends me into an orgasm like nothing I've ever felt before. He was right. I scream for him louder than I ever have. Spots dance in my vision, as the pleasure wracks through my body, as do the tremors.

I glance behind me, over my shoulder, and see him in a way I never have, but hope to again. He is stroking himself while he fingers me and, with a groan, comes all over my ass.

The feeling of contentment washes over me. I do this to him. Only me. I make him lose control, and get so turned on, he has to touch himself. It's a powerful and intoxicating feeling.

# Chapter Forty-Seven
## RAINA

Lorenzo comes into the bedroom as I finish getting ready. His gaze travels from my feet to my face, slowly.

"Fuck, Firecracker. Looks like I'm skipping my brother's wedding."

I place my hands on my hips and glare at him.

"We are not skipping Reaper and Bella's wedding."

He holds his finger up and does a circle motion, telling me to turn around.

Walking over to me, he runs his hand over my ass.

"Hear me out, Firecracker. We'll be a few minutes late. I'll get to fuck you, and we'll be there before they say 'I do'."

I turn to Lorenzo, who stands with his arms folded over his chest in mock annoyance.

"We are not skipping anything. Reaper would never forgive you."

He arches an eyebrow and shakes his head in disagreement.

"Reaper won't care, Raina. Guys don't care."

I step forward and take his hand. "Reaper cares a lot more than you guys think. Now let's go. I want to get there in time to see Bella before the ceremony."

He grumbles as we walk out the house together.

*Spoiled man child.*

He helps me into the passenger seat, leans down, and kisses me softly.

"You look beautiful, Firecracker."

"Thank you," I say, before he closes the door, comes around to the driver's side, and gets in.

"Do you remember the rules for the night?" He asks as he starts driving to Reaper's house, since they're having the wedding there. One of the perks to owning a mansion, I guess.

"Stay close to you. Only your brothers are to be trusted. And Bella, but she'll be busy," I answer easily, since he's been over the rules a hundred times already.

"Good girl," he says.

I glance over to him and ask, "All your brothers can be trusted? Even Psycho?"

He nods as he turns, driving us into the middle of nowhere. "Even Psycho. He won't hurt you. My oldest brother is unpredictable, but he wouldn't do that to himself. He knows better."

I'm not sure I completely trust Psycho, but I do trust Lorenzo, so I let it go.

"There will be other families there, so I need you to do as you're told for once."

I draw a circle with my finger over my head.

"I'm an angel."

He chuckles as he pulls onto a side road that appears to lead nowhere.

"Angel, my ass. Angel with devil horns maybe."

We pull up to a massive circular property with tall black gates around it, and I gasp audibly. I've seen nice houses, but this one is incredible. It looks like a damn castle.

He parks and walks me to the back of the building.

"Bella is in there. Tank will get you when you're ready. Text him."

We get out of the vehicle, and I throw my arms around his neck. Kissing me softly, he says, "I'll see you soon. Fucking behave."

I giggle as I walk in the door, but find Bella in tears.

220

"What's wrong?"

Athena comes in behind me and asks the same question.

"My dress won't zip up."

Athena and I share a glance, but then get to work getting the zipper up. It's tight, but not skin tight.

"Do I look fat?"

We both roll our eyes and tell her no.

She looks beautiful like she always does. Bella is wearing a sleeveless dress, with diamonds lining the 'V' neck. It falls to the floor and shows her body off perfectly, although her stomach isn't huge, but she's put on weight.

Placing her hands on her belly, she giggles.

"I guess the cat is out of the bag with this dress."

Athena and I stare at her, while she fixes her hair in the mirror.

"I'm pregnant. Again."

I fight back the tears threatening to fall, because I want this for her and Reaper. My family took their first child violently, and while this child won't bring him back, it's beautiful that they get this chance again.

"Congratulations," both Athena and I yell together.

Psycho knocks on the door and enters. I know Kage said not to be worried about him, but the sight of him brings on the nerves. If a man talks enough about wanting you dead, you fear him a bit.

"Ready, Bella?"

I stare in shock and she clearly catches it, because she says, "Psycho is walking me down the aisle. I don't really have a family."

They walk ahead of us, and Athena loops her arm in mine.

"They're very close."

"How did that happen?"

She rolls her eyes and giggles. "A shared love of knives and blood."

# Chapter Forty-Eight
## KAGE

Bella wanted an outdoor wedding, and if I've learned anything about my little brother's relationship, it's that Bella gets what she wants. I glance down the row of chairs beside me, and glance at my brother, Bones, holding onto Athena like she's a kite in a windstorm, not unlike the way I currently have my arm wrapped around Raina. Reaper stands at the makeshift altar, an archway covered in greenery, an assortment of flowers I know my girl had a part in, complete with twinkling lights.

His expression is intense as he waits for his bride, like at any moment he's going to sprint away and find his missing piece. The music starts and Bella comes into view, and my brother's face changes in an instant. Gone is the clenched jaw, and it's replaced with something I've never seen from him. Pure emotion.

Raina squeezes my thigh as Bella walks down the aisle, with Psycho escorting her. She looks stunning in a floor length white gown, diamonds lining the 'V' neck, while she carries red roses. She makes it halfway and stops walking, holding her hand to her chest and taking a deep breath, as Psycho says something in her ear. The emotion is thick in the air, as she makes it the rest of the way to my brother.

The dark brown wooden chairs are set up on the grass, with a dark red aisle runner on the ground. It's a small wedding, with about one hundred people attending. Reaper could've had hundreds here easily, but wanted to keep it on the smaller side to avoid issues. There are other families here, and he had to be careful about which ones to invite, to not cause problems. We get along with many of the other families. The Bonettis don't go looking for trouble, but if it shows up at our door, we will handle it. Our number one most profitable business is selling weapons to others in our world. Our manufacturer only sells to us, so if they want the guns of this caliber, there's nowhere else to get them.

Bella hands Psycho her flowers, which makes me chuckle softly. He kisses her on the cheek, and Raina coos an audible, "Aww."

My oldest brother would be very quick to tell you he doesn't have a heart, and doesn't give a fuck about anybody, but that's simply not true. In most cases, it is, but the crazy ass has a soft spot for Bella. She's different from most women we know. I think his insanity appreciates hers.

I hold Raina tighter, as we listen to Reaper and Bella say their vows.

"My living dead girl," Reaper says with a shake of his head, like he can't believe he's here.

"One look in your eyes changed my life. I must have been a better man in a past life to deserve you, because in this one, I don't. Even so, I'll keep you, protect you, and fucking love you like it's my goddamn job."

The disapproval flashes across the minister's face before he quickly hides it. Reaper holds Bella's hand, like he has to be touching her, and I know the feeling well.

She wipes a tear from her cheek as she takes a deep breath.

"Nico, you took a sad, unloved girl and made her whole. I don't say the word 'took' lightly," she says with a narrowed gaze, making those of us in the know laugh quietly.

"You crashed into my world, and destroyed everything I thought I knew about myself. I never knew love like this even existed. The kind of intensity that you'd burn the entire world down to keep. It's what we have. And I'd kill everyone in my way to keep it."

The minister rubs at his temple, as Raina pulls her bottom lip between her teeth, trying to stifle a giggle. I'm pretty sure that's the first time someone has referenced killing people in their vows, but that describes both Reaper and Bella to a 'T'.

"You may kiss the bride," the minister says, and I'm pretty sure he's relieved his part is done.

Reaper places his hands on Bella's face and lowers his head, capturing her lips with his. He kisses her like he's trying to suck the soul out of her, and maybe he is.

He takes her hand in his as the minister announces, "For the first time, I present to you, Mr. and Mrs. Bonetti."

Raina wipes a tear from her eye, as we watch them walk down the aisle as husband and wife, while I know my little brother confirmed something for me today.

Raina will be my wife.

We stand up, and I take her hand in mine.

"I want to show you something."

Walking to the other side of the property, she smiles as we make it to a massive garden.

"Oh my God. Reaper gardens?"

I chuckle softly.

"Definitely not, but his gardener does."

She walks around the different flowers, stopping to inhale their scents with a heavenly smile on her lips.

"Thank you for showing this to me," she says, and I pull her into my arms. I've been carrying this damn ring in my pocket for weeks, trying to figure out the perfect time. Maybe there isn't one, but there is a perfect woman, and she's it.

"Firecracker, I've been thinking about this for weeks now, trying to figure out how to do things perfectly, because you deserve that. You deserve a better man than me. Someone that knows all the right shit to say, but you'll have to settle for me, because I'll never let another man within a foot of you."

I clear my throat softly.

"The day I found you hiding from me was the best day of my life. I didn't know it then, but I do now. I'm never going to be a man that's gentle with you, because it's not who I am."

I dig into my pocket, as she stares at me with unshed tears in her eyes.

I open the ring box.

"Marry me, Raina. Become the Bonetti you are meant to be. Be mine for fucking eternity."

A soft smile forms on her lips and she speaks low, her voice filled with emotion, "Yes, Lorenzo, I'll marry you."

"Good," I say with a smirk, "It wasn't a request."

She rolls her eyes, feigning annoyance, but I already know she wouldn't have wanted a proposal with me on bended knee. That's not the man I am, and she takes me as I am. One of the many reasons I love her.

After placing the ten carat square diamond ring on her hand, I take her into my arms and kiss her. First it's slow and passionate, before it turns aggressive and desperate. My tongue slides against hers, as a moan escapes from her lips, making me ravenous for her. I pull back and stare at her, taking in all of her delicate features. Her green eyes sparkle under the moonlight as she places her hand on my cheek.

"I love you, Lorenzo."

"I love you too, Firecracker."

Raina Abruzzo was never supposed to be mine. She was from a rival family, and was meant to die with the rest of them, but with one look at her, I knew I had to take her. This woman knocked my entire world out of balance, and then righted it in a way only she could. Mafia men are not happy, but this is as close to it as it fucking gets for me. Like my brother and his new wife, I'd kill a million people if they stood in my way of Raina. Things change as the world turns, but one thing will always remain the same. She is mine.

The reception is coming to a close, as we stand with my brothers and their wives.

"Where the fuck is Psycho?" Bones asks.

I shrug, because I don't remember seeing him since the ceremony ended.

Raina looks at me with confusion as her phone starts ringing. She takes it out of her purse and stares at the phone in shock, as I see 'Psycho' flashing across the screen.

Where is my brother, and why the fuck is he calling Raina?

I take her cell from her hand and answer it on speakerphone.

"Where are you?" Bones asks.

"Doesn't matter," Psycho responds and then adds, "Raina, I'm sending you a picture, and need you to tell me if you recognize the person in the photo."

I open the message, and we all huddle around and look at the image.

A naked brunette woman is tied to a St. Andrew's Cross with rope. Blood drips down her thighs, and the expression on her face is one of extreme horror. Something only Psycho can provide.

"That's the ADA. That's Anastasia Crowne," Raina gasps.

"Oh, little lamb. You lied about who you are," he says, his voice dripping with evil.

Bones says, "Psycho, you cannot fucking kidnap the Assistant District Attorney."

My brother responds plainly.

"You're wrong, Bones. I already did."

And the line goes dead.

# EPILOGUE
## RAINA

*One Year Later…*

Unlike Reaper and Bella, we didn't want a wedding with a bunch of people around, so we got married just the two of us, with only his brothers and their wives present. It was perfect and only about us. Since we have a new baby, I didn't have the energy to plan a big event. One thing you don't realize, before having children, is that they are simply exhausting.

*And perfect.*

Athena holds our son while Lorenzo takes my hands in his, as we stand near the rock waterfall at Bones' house. It's quiet and peaceful as the water splashes against the rocks.

"My beautiful Firecracker. One year ago my life began. You came into my life like a hurricane, threatening to destroy everything in its path. And you did. Raina, you were my destruction, and now you're my salvation. You give me everything I need, before I even know I need it. I don't deserve you, but I will spend the rest of my life keeping your heart safe. I will love you and protect you with everything I have."

A tear rolls down my cheek as I take in a shaky breath.

"Lorenzo, I thought the worst thing that would ever happen to me was you finding me. It was the best thing, because you helped me find myself. I never knew love. Not like this."

I shake my head in disbelief.

"You're a better man than you think you are, at least with me, and with our son. Thank you for loving me in a way I never believed anyone could."

The minister pronounces us husband and wife, and Lorenzo places his hands on my face, as if waiting for this has caused him excruciating pain. He growls into my mouth.

"Mine," and pushes his tongue inside my mouth, kissing me aggressively, just the way I like. My husband is not sweet or gentle. He's intense and perfect.

I turn to see our son in Athena's arms and go to grab him, but she shakes her head no.

"Kiss him, and go enjoy time with your new husband. I promise he's in good hands."

Looking around for someone to back me up, I get none. Bella is holding their son Maddox, and Reaper is holding his twin, Axel.

She shakes her head and says, "We are all going to take good care of Greyson."

*Twins.*

I'm very happy for her and Reaper, but I'm good with one at a time.

"Say goodnight, Firecracker."

I kiss our son on the head, our sweet little Grey, and sigh softly. There isn't a day that goes by that I don't wish my mom could've held him, at least once. Lorenzo had her buried in the Bonetti cemetery when I was held in the basement. I didn't like that he made the decision, but I'm glad she's close by. Some days I sit out there for hours with her, simply talking about everything and nothing. I don't blame him for her death, because I know it was accidental, but when I look at our son, I miss her so much it physically hurts. Grey squeezes my hand, like he knows the thoughts going through my head, and he's offering me comfort. I smile at him softly, this little man changed me for the better. Both my men did. It's funny how life can change in a moment. A bad thing can turn everything around.

"Firecracker," Lorenzo growls impatiently.

I give Grey another kiss on the forehead, as he stares at me like his world begins and ends with me.

"I love you. Mommy will see you in the morning."

Lorenzo kisses him on the cheek.

"Make sure you keep Uncle Bones and Aunt Athena up all night long, like we talked about."

Bones shakes his head with a groan, and Lorenzo pulls me away from our son, because he knows if he gives me the choice, I'll never leave.

You know you can fall in love with a man, but I never expected to fall head over heels in love with the child I honestly didn't think I wanted. The moment I held him for the first time, I knew I had a love for him different from anything I've ever experienced. He is an unexpected gift.

Lorenzo helps me into the car, and slides in beside me with a grin.

"What are you up to?"

"Tonight, I'm taking what's mine."

He's talking about my ass. I don't have to question it, because I know it's the one thing he wants and has never had, aside from his fingers. I'm a little worried because he's huge.

"Still trust me, Firecracker?"

A nervous smile forms on my lips as I nod.

"I do."

I'm terrified, but also know my husband will take care of me. He always does.

BOOK FOUR

# Psycho

A DARK MAFIA ROMANCE

## CHELLE ROSE

Anastasia Crowne is the name that both Bones and Kage gave to me for this Assistant District Attorney. I watch her smile, and collect her coffee from the register of Mounds Coffee Company, which I happen to think is a poorly named business. She smiles and laughs with the man at the counter, completely fucking oblivious to the man watching her.

Her killer.

I'm not Reaper. I don't go searching for people to kill because their eyes look interesting when they die. I'm also not fucking pussy whipped like my three brothers are either. Apparently, if they are a good enough fuck, we let traitors live. I cannot touch Kage's firecracker, but the woman that started it all? She's as good as fucking dead.

I lick my lips as I watch the woman carry on with her life, as if she has nothing but time.

*Pretty little lamb, you should not have gone into the wolf's den.*

She wanted to know more about the Bonetti Brothers. Her wish is my command. The pretty little counselor will learn first hand that you do not fuck with us.

*One, two, Psycho is coming for you.*
*Three, four, your blood will coat my floor.*
*Five, six, you'll beg to live.*
*Seven, eight, it's too late.*
*Nine, ten, scream for me again.*

# ACKNOWLEDGEMENTS

My tiny alpha team grew a lot with this book. Beta readers are so important for authors and I'm honored to have had a wonderful group helping me make my book better.

Heather, DiDi, Nikki, Crystal, Panda, Steph, and Grace, thank you for reading Kage before it was even complete. Every comment made this book better. The way you have loved the Bonetti Brothers warms my heart. Thank you.

A special note to Grace Farnsworth. You are not only my PA, you're my everything. I have never heard the words, 'that's not in your contract.' If I need it, you're there. I've said it before and I'll say it again, I don't know how I'd do this without you. I don't want to find out. Love you to the moon and back. Codeword: Basement.

Thank you to the reader for taking a chance on my words and making my dreams come true.
Furious Editing thank you as always for taking such great care of my words and lack of commas. Love you!

RedFox Book Design: thank you for the amazing covers. These are my favorites because you know… hot men.

# ALSO BY CHELLE ROSE:

**Forbidden Desires Series**

1. *Mercy www.books2read.com/chellerosemercy*
2. *Finding Mercy www.books2read.com/chellerosefinding-mercy*
3. *Liam and Mercy www.books2read.com/LiamandMercy*
4. *Xander's Secret https://books2read.com/Xanderssecret*

**Dark Desires Series**

1. *Unholy www.books2read.com/chelleroseunholy*
2. *Unhinged www.books2read.com/chelleroseunhinged*
3. *Unchained www.books2read.com/chelleroseunchained*
4. *Undone www.books2read.com/chelleroseundone*
5. *An Unhinged Wedding www.books2read.com/unhingedwedding*

**Men of Mayhem Series**

1. *De Luca: The Devil* www.books2read.com/delucathedevil
2. *De Luca: The Saint* www.books2read.com/delucasaint
3. *De Luca: The Sinister Game* www.books2read.com/sinistergame
4. De Luca: The Dalia Effect www.books2read.com/thedaliaeffect

**Den of Sin Duet**

1. Zade www.books2read.com/zade
2. Sin www.books2read.com/sin-chellerose

## Bonetti Brothers Series

1. Bones www.books2read.com/boneschellerose
2. Reaper www.books2read.com/reaper-chellerose
3. Kage www.books2read.com/kage-chellerose
4. Psycho www.books2read.com/psycho-chellerose

Printed in Dunstable, United Kingdom

68187915R00139